Lakefronts and Larceny

A Sweetwater Springs Southern Mystery

S.C. Merritt

Published by Sarah Merritt, 2020.

ONE

"**G**irl, we look good." I commented, as I leaned across the glass-topped bakery display case and spread out the latest copy of the Sweetwater Herald. The photo splashed across the front page showed my daughter, Macy, grinning from ear to ear, her boyfriend, Antonio Castellini, and me, a very proud mom. Several members of the Sweetwater Springs Chamber of Commerce stood alongside us, looking on as the Mayor used a gigantic pair of scissors to cut the ribbon, symbolizing the Grand Opening of Macy's On Main, Hometown Bakery and Beanery. After months of tearing out wood paneling, refinishing original hardwood floors, installing a state-of-the-art commercial baking kitchen and a plethora of cappuccino, espresso and coffee appliances, her dream had become a reality. I was so proud of my girl that I could bust wide open.

Macy had just brought out a warm pan of made-from-scratch, blueberry biscuits and was arranging them on a tray for the morning rush. "We look awesome except for that goofy grin on my face!" she commented, as she drizzled the warm sugar glaze over the biscuits. "Why do I have to show every tooth in my mouth?"

"I think it's a great picture," I said as I took a bite of the warm biscuit and groaned in delight. "And how cool is it that soon there'll be a picture of Tony's ribbon cutting for Tavolo? The grand opening of two new eateries in Sweetwater Springs in the same month must be the biggest thing to happen here since the county seceded from the state during the Civil War," I said, referring to the history that was our town and county's claim to fame. When the State of Alabama seceded from the Union, our county was so opposed to the Confederacy, it seceded from the state. There was even a big statue of a soldier dressed half in Confederate uniform, and half in Union standing in the center of town to commemorate the event.

"I'm so excited for both of us. A little scared, but excited." Macy confided. "He's been so good to help me even with his own place opening in a couple of weeks."

Macy's former chef instructor, and now, boyfriend, had volunteered to come over from Mississippi back in May and help her with her bakery design and menu planning. Over the last few months, not only had he fallen in love with the town, but it seemed he might be falling in love with Macy. As they worked together on her bakery and coffee shop plans, he got the idea to purchase the storefront next door and open an Italian restaurant.

From the little information I could drag out of Macy, this wasn't the first time he had owned his own place. Tony had been co-owner in a restaurant somewhere up north several years ago but made the decision to leave the restaurant business to teach culinary school. I guess he was ready to give it another shot. He was quite a bit older than Macy. It took me a while to get used to the idea that he was closer to my age than to hers. But it didn't take me long to see what she saw in him. He had such a kind and generous heart. It was easy to see that he cared for and believed in Macy. They supported each other in their new business ventures, and it was going to be fun to see where their relationship went.

I walked over to the coffee area and poured myself a large iced coffee to go. "I hate to leave you, but I need to head on in to work. Nana should be here any minute to help you out."

Macy peeked around the half-open swinging door to the kitchen. "I just put the last of the dark chocolate pound cakes in to bake. Once she gets here, she can start mixing up the cranberry pecan crisps, and I'll work out front."

The bakery had only been open a couple of weeks, and we knew Macy couldn't afford to pay anyone to help just yet, so Momma and I were tag teaming. She worked on Monday and Wednesday, the days I worked in the office at Sweetwater Springs Baptist Church, and I planned to work with Macy on the other days. From the conversations I'd had with Momma, she seemed to be a little overwhelmed. "How is she doing with her barista lessons?" I yelled, as I straightened tables and chairs across the room.

Macy came through the door wiping her hands on her apron. "Pretty good. I don't think she expected it to be as complicated as it is, but she's actually catching on pretty quickly." She flipped the switch on both coffeemakers.

"I can sympathize with her. Some of these machines are complicated and it seems that these days it's become more of an art form!"

The bell over the door jingled and Momma flipped the sign on the door to OPEN as she came breezing in. "Mornin' Macy! Mornin' Glory!" Momma beamed. Everyone got such a kick out of greeting me that way, including Momma.

"Well, you sound chipper for a Monday morning!" I laughed.

"Good morning, Nana. Do you mind working on some cookies in the kitchen?"

"I'll do whatever helps you the most," Momma said, tying an apron around her waist and heading through the swinging door with a smile of complete relief. Momma was well-known for being one of the best cooks in town. The cooking gene skipped a generation with me, but I was glad Macy got it.

The door jingled again, as Megan Lester, and a lady I didn't recognize, came in dressed to the nines and browsed the pastry selection in the display case.

"Good morning ladies! What can I get for you this morning?" Macy chirped. "The blueberry biscuits are to die for, if I do say so myself."

"I'll take one of those and a skinny vanilla latte," Megan responded.

Megan was the president of our local Ladies' Club and Southern to the core. My Granny would say that she always "put on the dog," which meant she acted a little uppity. When I first met Megan, I thought the same thing. But the more I'd gotten to know her, the more I realized she was just a true Southern belle. She had a kind heart and had never been anything but nice to me. She and the other ladies had welcomed me into the Ladies' Club with open arms. Maybe they saw me as new blood, and it probably helped that I had a problem saying *no* and usually regretted it later. I had gotten in over my head on several occasions, one of which I was in the middle of now.

"I think I'll go with the chocolate croissant and a cup of whatever your boldest roast coffee is this morning," Megan's friend said as they took a seat at one of the bistro tables on the other side of the room.

Even standing at the counter several feet away, I could still hear bits and pieces of their conversation. The lady with Megan was clearly adamant about something and Megan kept nodding her head like she was agreeing with her. I heard the word *condo*, and my radar immediately went on full alert. Construction on a group of resort condominiums called Pine Bluffs was just getting underway out on Smith Lake. Although many people in town were excited about the potential it had to bring in the tourist trade, there was a pocket of citizens who were adamantly against it. These were mostly made up of lakefront landowners whose property was near the resort.

Macy arranged the blueberry biscuit and chocolate croissant on cute, mismatched, vintage dessert plates and placed them on a serving tray on the counter along with their coffee orders. I took the opportunity to get a little closer to the conversation and delivered the delicious goodies myself.

"I don't know about you and Chris, but Jeff and I are not going to stand for it," the other lady said. "Our property values have already taken a hit, and they've barely broken ground."

Megan nodded. "Believe me, Chris feels the same way. We need to do *whatevah* it takes to get this project stopped before it goes any *fuh-tha*," Megan continued in her Scarlett O'Hara southern drawl. "Don't you worry your sweet little head. I have a feeling we won't have that little problem much *longa, dahling*."

"Here you go, ladies. Best breakfast in town!" I smiled as I placed the plates in front of them along with their coffees.

"This smells just divine!" Megan exclaimed. "Macy is as sweet as tea, and this place is just heavenly. I know it's gonna be a glorious success."

"Thanks, Megan. I'm pretty proud of her." I smiled and turned to the other lady as she took her first bite of the croissant and groaned in delight. "I don't think we've met. My name is Glory Harper. I'm Macy's mom. I'm in the Ladies' Club with Megan."

"Oh, Glory, I do apologize! I thought you had met Cindy," Megan said, placing her hand daintily on the other lady's arm. "This is Cindy Newsome. She is in the Ladies' Club with us. She and her husband Jeff own Hearth and Home Furniture."

"Nice to meet you, Glory. Since summer is our slowest time for sales, we use that time to travel to trade shows and furniture markets to get ready for the fall, which is our busiest time of year. I have had to miss the last few meetings. I hate missing out on all the fun, but business comes before anything else at our house." Cindy smiled, but I noticed the smile didn't quite reach her blue eyes.

"I didn't mean to eavesdrop," I said, with my fingers crossed behind my back, "but I couldn't help overhearing your conversation about the condo project. I know Megan's position on it, but I take it that you and your husband are opposed to it also?"

I knew Megan and Chris Lester were one hundred percent against the project. They lived on the Upper End of the lake. That's where the condos were being built. Commercial buildings like the boat docks, bait store, jet ski rentals, Lakeside Motel and Lake House Café were all much further down the shoreline. A few months ago, Megan had commented to me that Terrance Wolfe had better "watch his back" if he tried to move forward with the project.

"Yes. We live next to Megan and Chris on the Upper End and are just as concerned as everyone else that the commercial rentals will destroy our property values. And let's not forget the ambiance on the Upper End that we paid a pretty penny to acquire." Cindy lifted her coffee cup to take a drink with her pinky finger stuck out a mile.

"I see. I can understand your concerns, but don't you feel like the beauty of our lake is something that everyone should be able to enjoy? God's beauty in nature really belongs to everyone, right? Hopefully, this will boost the economy of our town and as a result your furniture business will grow."

"Maybe," Cindy frowned and shrugged as she took another sip of her coffee.

"Well, ladies, I hope you have a wonderful day. I need to get moving if I'm going to make it to the church office on time." I returned the serving tray to Macy at the counter, told her I'd see her tonight and headed to work.

TWO

Sweetwater Springs Baptist Church was only a few blocks over from Main Street. School was back in session, and the streets were busy this morning with school buses and people headed to work. I drove down Main, turned onto Sycamore Street and then pulled into the church parking lot. I had been excited to find a part-time job after moving back to my hometown from Texas not quite a year ago. The office was only open two days a week, and I took care of all the general office work in addition to membership records and financials. So far, it had been more work than I anticipated and not as low-stress as I had hoped, especially after a murder was committed right in my office during one of the biggest church services of the year. It had taken me a while to feel comfortable coming back into the office to work, but each day it was getting a little easier. I was pretty proud of the fact that I, along with Momma, Macy and my sister-in-law Kelly had helped bring the killer to justice. Of course, my brother, Detective Jake Miller, was not a fan of our little Crime Club, as we called it. Neither was his boss, Chief Detective Hunt Walker.

I met Chief Walker for the first time when I was called in for questioning and fingerprinting during the murder investigation. The fact that the murder weapon belonged to me didn't help the situation. Jake assured me I was never really a suspect, but I still took it personally, or at least, I let him believe I did, just to watch him squirm. Thanks to my well-meaning, matchmaking family, Chief Walker and I had conveniently found ourselves thrown together on several occasions over the last few months, and I had to admit, I didn't hate it. He was extremely handsome, in a salt and pepper, rugged kind of way.

In the two years since my late husband Dave's death, I had been so focused on the investigation, I hadn't put much effort into a social life. It had been a long time since I'd looked at anyone besides Dave, and I had certainly never taken any passing comments seriously, if any came my way at all. But this man was different. I got this weird feeling when we were in the same room. He had flirted with me on several occasions. At least, I thought he was flirting. There was one day when a group of us went on a picnic down by the lake. I had turned my ankle the previous day, so when everyone else went for a trail hike, I stayed behind. After about five minutes, he returned and sat down on the blanket next to me. We laughed and enjoyed each other's company. I could see in his steel gray eyes that he was thinking of kissing me. My heart was pounding, but my mind wasn't sure I was ready for it. He leaned in closer and I let my eyes close. Just when our lips were about to meet, a yellow jacket came out of nowhere and attacked me. I swatted at it and accidently slapped him in the side of the head. I was mortified. While I was apologizing, the darned thing came back and stung me right on the lip. I'd never been so embarrassed in my life. After recovering from the clobbering I gave him, Hunt got some ice for my lip, as it swelled at an astronomical rate. By the time the rest of the group returned, I looked like a duck-billed platypus. I figured after that fiasco, he'd had enough of my craziness.

Actually, I didn't have time for him or any other distractions in my life at the moment. I must have been crazy to let myself get roped into heading up the Sweetwater Springs Ladies Club Annual Purse Auction by default. I only volunteered to assist with the auction, but Stephanie Bramlett, the member originally in charge, had gone into labor a month early and left me to take the reins. Organizing the auction, along with my job at the church and helping Macy at the bakery, had me with too many irons in the fire, as Granny always said. I pushed each project back into its own little compartment in my brain and focused on the job at hand.

"Mornin' Glory!" Pastor Dan greeted, as I settled in at my desk and booted up my computer.

"Good Morning!" I saw that the counting team was here right on time and already at work.

Being a retired math teacher and gifted with a head for numbers, Momma had served on the team of church members who counted the offering on Monday mornings and delivered the deposit to the bank for several years. But when she began helping Macy at the bakery, she had resigned her spot on the team and Janice Fleming had taken her place. Janice was a retired certified public accountant and still did a little bookkeeping on the side for a couple of small businesses. One of those happened to be owned by Sam Baylor, one of our newest church members. Sam had taken up permanent residence in Sweetwater Springs a few months back and had turned out to be a huge asset to the community. He came to town to look at some family property and then, by sheer accident, found out he had a son. Talk about a surprise visit!

"Good morning. Glad you went ahead and started without me," I said, as I peeked into the counting room to greet Janice and Larry Griffin, the third member of the team. "Got a lot of things on my plate and I feel like I'm running around like a chicken with my head cut off."

Janice laughed, "Girl, you need to slow down and take a breather! That daughter of yours has it all under control. She's doing a great job. I went by Saturday and picked up a dessert for Sunday lunch, and it was divine!"

"You're right. I know she can do it. I guess it's just a mom thing. Helping her with the bakery and heading up the purse auction has me tired already."

"That reminds me," Janice interjected, "I have several purses to donate to the purse auction. I need to go straight from here to the office at the condo worksite. If I run by the house and pick them up, do you think you would have time to stop by the construction office and grab them?"

"I'd be glad to. I can run out there on my lunch hour. It's been a while since I've driven by, and I'd love to see the progress on the condos."

"Great! If I'm not there, I'll leave them in a bag with your name on it just inside the office door. Terrance and I have a meeting at the mayor's office at some point today. They haven't said what time. After the big ruckus at the last city council meeting, I hope we can get all the differences ironed out between Terrance and the lake landowners. If they don't come to a compromise soon, some people are going to lose a lot of money." She turned back to her counting duties. "Thanks again, Glory!"

When Terrance Wolfe, owner of Sweetwater Springs Realty and Rentals, purchased a large chunk of prime lakefront real estate from Sam Baylor, he asked Sam, an architect, to come on board with the project as lead designer. Sam jumped at the chance to relocate to Sweetwater Springs and be closer to the woman and son he loved.

Lunchtime rolled around, and I went through the drive-thru at Moody's Lunchbox to grab a burger and an iced tea, then headed out of town toward the lake. It was a windy, but beautiful day, so I figured I would find a nice spot to pull off with a scenic view of the lake and enjoy lunch before I picked up the purses from Janice. Sure enough, I spotted an empty picnic table at the overlook, so I quickly ate while I watched some boaters and wakeboarders enjoying the last few weeks on the lake. Before too long, the water would be too cold, and everyone would hang up their skis until next summer.

Pulling up to the mobile unit that housed the construction office, the first thing I noticed was an unusually quiet and almost deserted parking lot. I was expecting a noisy, busy construction site. I didn't see Janice's car anywhere. In fact, the only car in the parking lot was a very expensive-looking sports car. I don't know cars, and I can't tell you one make from another, but I know money when I see it, and this one was worth a lot of it. It had a New York vanity plate that read, HNDSOFF.

Following Janice's instructions, I walked up the steps to the door marked OFFICE and knocked. I assumed that the owner of the flashy car was probably in the office. Getting no answer, I tried the knob. The grimy knob turned in my hand, and I swung the door open and took a step inside. The office was empty, but sure enough, there sat the bag of purses with my name on a yellow sticky note attached to it. I glanced around and called out in case there was someone in the back.

"Hello? Anybody here?" Again, no answer, so I grabbed the bag and headed out of the office and back toward my car. As I wrangled the black trash bag full of purses into my back seat, a familiar truck pulled into the gravel lot and stopped next to mine. I shut the door to my Honda and turned to greet Sam.

"Hey, Glory! What are you doing out here?" He met me with a smile.

"I came by to pick up some purses that Janice is donating for the Ladies' Club Purse Auction, but she must have already left for her meeting with the mayor. No one's inside the office, so I just grabbed them. Hope that's okay."

"No problem. Did you meet Gino? I see his car is here."

"No, but that's some kinda nice car. Who's Gino?"

"He's our main investor from New York. I guess you noticed that there's no work being done here today. I think Terrance said there's been a hold up with some of the permit approvals from the city. It's a shame since we barely got started, and every day we don't work, we're having to pay workers anyway. Maybe he's out on the site looking around. Do you have time to take a walk with me? I'd like to introduce you to Gino. He's a character, for sure. Kind of intimidating, though. We've been joking that he's got mob connections. I'm not sure where his money comes from, but he's got plenty of it."

"I'd love to see the progress. How did Terrance get hooked up with this Gino guy? We don't have a lot of big money, New York connections around here." I laughed.

"I think the new guy in town, that's opening that Italian restaurant, introduced them."

"What?" My face paled and I jerked around to face Sam. "Tony knows this guy?"

Something uneasy churned in my stomach. Why would my daughter's boyfriend have connections to big money in New York? How much did Macy really know about Tony's past? Immediately, I started talking myself down off the ledge. *What's the big deal? Lots of rich people have totally legitimate and legal jobs. I'm sure there is a simple explanation.*

"Is Tony the restaurant guy?" Sam asked.

"Yes, and my daughter is kind of dating him." I looked at Sam. "Should I be worried?"

"Nah, Gino seems like a nice enough guy. At least wait till you meet him and be the judge for yourself. He's probably over at ground zero, which is what will be the main entrance for the resort lobby."

He pointed to a canopy-covered area about fifty yards away. I followed Sam as we trudged our way through the site, stepping over debris and around stacks of building materials covered by tarps to protect them from the elements.

"Gino? Are you here?" Sam cupped his hands around his mouth and yelled at the top of his lungs.

The only sound we heard in response was the lapping of the water on the lakeshore about two hundred yards away and the snapping of the tarps in the wind. Something caught my eye behind a stack of lumber when a huge gust of wind blew the tarp straight up in the air. We rushed to grab the tarp and secure it. It was then we saw why it had been disturbed. A pair of very expensive, Italian loafers stuck out from under the other side. I screamed and I heard my echo all the way across the lake.

Sam stumbled backwards and fell on the ground, while I tried to steady myself against a nearby tree in the strong wind.

"Oh no! This looks bad! Call 911, Glory, and I'll see if he's still alive."

"No!" I screamed as Sam bent over to check for a pulse.

He jerked up and looked at me wide-eyed. "Why?"

"I'm sorry! I didn't mean to scream at you. Just be really careful not to disturb the body or touch anything if you don't have to. If he's already dead, which I'm assuming he is from that bullet hole in his forehead, we don't want to mess up the crime scene." I pulled out my cell phone, scrolled down to find Jake's number and called.

THREE

"Hey, Sis. What's up?"

"Uh, well . . ." my voice trailed off.

"Glory, what is it? What's wrong?"

"I think you need to get to the new condo construction site as soon as you can. Sam and I just found a dead body." I cringed, dreading his reaction.

"Are you okay? Are you hurt? Was it a construction accident?"

"I'm fine. And no, not unless he accidentally crawled under a tarp and shot himself in the forehead."

"On my way. Do not move."

I couldn't bear to look at poor Gino, so paced around, looking anywhere but at the body.

The ground and surrounding area was trampled down just like any construction site would be with dozens of boot prints. One thing that was conspicuously missing, though, was blood. Other than the trickle coming from the gaping hole right between the eyes, there wasn't any that I could see. That told me one thing. Secondary crime scene. Jake would be here soon, so I knew I probably only had about five minutes to look around without being told to stay out of the way. I took the opportunity to snap some pictures. I knew Momma, Macy and Kelly would want the lowdown as soon as I was able to talk to them.

Sam was on his phone, presumably to Terrance, informing him of what was going on. I took a few pictures of the body and the area around the tarp. Then I nonchalantly walked around the general area to see if I could spot anything unusual or out of place. As far as I could tell, there was no sign of a murder weapon. Even if the killer didn't take the gun with them, there would be a million places here on a huge worksite to hide it, including a hundred-acre lake just yards away. It would be like finding a needle in a haystack, and I didn't envy Jake that job.

I walked back toward the parking lot where my car was parked. I took special care to only step where Sam and I had already walked. Jake would be furious if I contaminated the crime scene. There was a second path from the way that Sam and I walked. It looked like a more direct route leading to the back door of the office. I could hear sirens in the distance, so without venturing any further, I looked toward the back door of the office. It was about twenty feet away, but even from that distance, there appeared to be footprints in the loose gravel and a definite pattern of drag marks. I couldn't see how far it went, but I would be willing to bet it started at the base of the steps leading to the back door of the trailer and led straight to the location of the body. I hurried back to the general area where Sam was still on the phone, pacing back and forth frantically, just as Jake's department-issued truck skidded to a stop in the gravel lot. The ambulance and two other official vehicles followed close behind. I cringed as I watched Hunt Walker get out of one of them and shut the truck door. He glanced around the parking lot and then spotted me. Our eyes locked and he made a beeline in my direction. His boots crunching in the gravel, he never took his eyes off me.

"Afternoon, Chief Walker. I can explain..." my voice trailed off.

"I know you will, and I'm looking forward to hearing that explanation, but I need to see the scene first. Come with me."

I walked alongside him as we trudged through the worksite toward where Jake and the medical examiner were taking a closer look at the victim.

"So, I'm thinking that whatever happened to this guy, didn't happen out here. I think it must have happened in the office." I said, beginning to get out of breath trying to keep up with his long strides.

"Why am I not surprised that you already have a theory? What makes you think that?" he said, still walking full stride.

"I saw drag marks." He stopped and turned to stare at me. I tried not to look like I was sucking wind like a vacuum cleaner.

"Where?"

I pointed toward the back door to the trailer, still trying to level out my breathing. "And there's not much blood."

He let out an exasperated grunt and took off at a full sprint toward Jake, leaving me in his dust.

As I got closer to the scene, I could see Jake directing a group of uniformed officers to cordon off the area around the entire perimeter of the trailer, front and back. A team took pictures of the path between the back door and the body. I decided I'd better call Pastor Dan at the church office to let him know I wouldn't be back today. Thank goodness I had gotten all the pressing items on my to-do list completed before I left for lunch. The rest could wait until Wednesday. Just as I was disconnecting that call, someone touched me on the elbow, and I jumped. Hunt was standing behind me so close I could feel his breath on my neck.

"Are you okay, Glory?"

"Yes, I'm fine. I just needed to call the office to let them know I wouldn't be back in today. I didn't give any details."

"I appreciate that. We would like to keep the panic down to a minimum in town as long as we can."

I nodded and turned to face him.

"Could you answer some questions for me now? Jake is taking Sam's statement, so I guess you're stuck with me." He smiled and I saw the hint of a dimple.

I nodded and covered a fake cough trying to hide an unexpected flush in my cheeks.

"Okay, start from the beginning. What are you doing out here with Sam Baylor in the middle of the day at a deserted work site?"

I hoped that the stink-eye I gave him let him know how much I did not appreciate that innuendo.

"First of all, I'm old enough to be Sam's moth— older sister, and Sam wasn't here when I first arrived. We didn't come out here together."

"Okay, okay. Sorry. It was a bad attempt at humor. I know you weren't up to anything seedy," he said with an apologetic smile. "Please start from the beginning."

"Janice Fleming is now on our counting team, since Momma started helping Macy in the bakery. When she came in to count this morning, she told me she had some purses she wanted to donate to the Ladies' Club purse auction and asked if I could run by here and pick them up. I agreed, and said I'd come out on my lunch break. She said if she had to leave before I arrived, she'd leave the bag in the office. When I got here, there was no one in the office, so I saw the bag with my name on it and took it to my car."

"There was no one at all in the office or anywhere that you could see?"

"No. I called out and got no answer, so I just picked up the bag and left."

"What about the car in the parking lot? Was it here when you arrived?"

"Yes. That's why I thought there might be someone in the office, but there wasn't."

"Okay, go on."

"That's when Sam drove up. He saw the car and asked me if I had met Gino. He said the car belonged to Gino, who was one of the main investors for the project."

Hunt's brow furrowed like he was deep in thought. "Did he say anything else about this Gino? Last name, maybe?"

"No last name, but he did say they were always joking around the office that he had mob connections since he was from New York."

"Mob? That's just great. That's all we need here in the middle of nowhere. A mob hit."

"He was just joking. Surely, it was just because his name was Gino and that sounds so mobbish."

"Mobbish? Really? I don't think that's a thing." In spite of the circumstances, he stifled a laugh.

"Whatever. I'm sure there's no way that could be true because Macy's boyfriend, Tony, is the one who introduced them to Gino. Tony's a great guy. He wouldn't know the mob if they..." My voice caught in my throat.

"Hit him right between the eyes?" Hunt finished the old cliché. I swallowed down the worry rising and nodded.

"What happened next?" he asked.

"So, anyway, Sam asked me if I wanted to meet Gino and see the progress on the construction. I said that would be nice, so I walked with him out to the site. That's when the wind blew up the corner of the tarp and I saw the feet sticking out. I'm thinking that he was killed in the trailer and then dragged out here. Someone had obviously tried to hide Gino and didn't get the tarp secured well enough." I realized I'd been rattling on and stopped to take a breath.

"Let's not jump to any conclusions just yet. You didn't touch anything, did you?"

I rolled my eyes. "Of course not. I even made sure Sam didn't touch the body." I felt like I was having a serious case of déjà vu, flashing back to the body in the cemetery I had discovered a few months ago.

"Okay, I guess that's all I need right now. Will you be okay to get back to town alone?" He smiled that smile again. The one with the little dimple.

"I'm fine. Let me know if you need any more information, or if you need me to help in any way," I said, as innocently as I could.

Now it was his turn to roll his eyes. "Sure, Sherlock. I'll be sure to let you know," he said with a wink.

FOUR

The first thing on my mind was to talk to Macy. I knew she was probably busy at the bakery, or at least I hoped that she was busy, so that would have to wait until later. I don't know if she knew more about Tony's background than she had told me, or if she was just as much in the dark as I was. I really wanted to know just how Tony was connected to Gino.

I decided to swing by the library and see if Kelly had time to help me find out more about Gino and his investment company. Kelly had recently made the decision, after a short stint in the corporate sector, that she wasn't cut out for the business world, so she put her Computer Science degree to work at our local library. I thought it was a perfect fit. She had always loved books, and so much research is done at the library, she was the perfect one to help the online novice. She could find any information you needed in no time flat. I walked through the double glass doors and scanned the room until I saw Kelly in the fiction section. She was placing the last of a cartful of books back on the shelves. She looked up and motioned toward the main desk, letting me know she would meet me there.

I made my way to the big octagonal desk in the center of the room and waited, trying to keep my imagination in check. I could jump to conclusions faster than a jackrabbit in a dog pen. One of my many character flaws. I'd always been a bit of a worrier, but after my late husband, Dave was killed, worry ran amuck in my brain if I didn't keep it in check. It didn't take much to send my imagination into a tailspin. Dave had been a steady rock in my life since we started dating in high school. I needed to cut myself some slack. In the last two years, I had become a stronger, more self-sufficient woman. I was still a work in progress, but I was pretty proud of how far I'd come.

Kelly opened the latch on the little half door that allowed employees behind the desk, slipped through, and clicked it closed.

"Hey, Glory! What are you doing here in the middle of the afternoon? Didn't you work today?"

I knew it had only been about an hour since Sam made the 911 call, but I was relieved that the news hadn't made it all over town yet. "I take it you haven't heard about the incident at the lake condo site?" I raised an eyebrow as she looked at me and slowly shook her head back and forth.

"Noooo," she said, drawing the word out. "Did something bad happen?"

"I kind of found another body." I whispered, realizing there were patrons in the general area.

"You what?!" Kelly scream-whispered, if that's a thing. "How does this happen to you? That's three, Glory! THREE!"

"You think I don't know that? I don't know why it's always me. Just lucky, I guess," I said sarcastically and proceeded to tell her the whole story: how the wind blew the tarp up and showed us Gino's million-dollar loafers and then how Hunt took my statement.

"Did he smile that killer smile with the dimple?" she waggled her eyebrows.

"Stop it!" I whispered and gave her a playful slap on the arm. "To answer the question that you are about to ask, I am not trying to get involved in any investigation. I was just curious about who this guy is that got himself shot. Do you have time to do some quick research for me?"

Kelly gave me a smile that said she didn't believe a word I just said. "Sure, what do you need?" she asked, already settling in behind her computer monitor.

Still whispering, I said, "First of all, see if you can find a list of investors in the Pine Bluffs Condominium project. I'm specifically looking for our unfortunate dead guy's last name. All I know is his first name is Gino, and I think he's from New York. Anything you can find on his background would be great." I felt someone come up behind me. A little elderly lady shuffled up with a stack of books so high, I could barely see her gray hair all piled on top of her head. She must've just come from Bonnie June's for her weekly set and comb out. I smiled as I stepped out of her way and helped her hoist the stack up onto the counter.

"I need to take care of a few more things here at work, and I'll swing by tonight to let you know what I find," Kelly said, as she reached for the lady's books.

I knew I needed to talk to Momma and Macy soon. They would both be livid if they heard the news of the murder from anyone but me. I started the car and glanced at the clock on the dash. The bakery closed at three, and it was already two thirty. I decided to head on over there and fill them in.

I could see from the stink eye I received from Momma when I walked through the door, that they had already heard the news.

"Mom, are you alright?" Macy exclaimed. "Bonnie June came by a few minutes ago and told us something bad happened out at the condo construction site, and that you were there." Bonnie June Dixon owned Bonnie's Cut and Curl on Main Street. It was right next door to Sweetwater Springs Realty and Rentals and was well known as the gossip mothership. Anything important in town usually went through Bonnie's place first. Bonnie June was one of Momma's best friends.

"What's going on and why were you out there in the middle of the day?" Macy came at me with a barrage of questions.

"And why are we just now hearing from you? I was worried and you didn't answer your phone," Momma scolded.

I dug my phone out of the bottom of my purse, and, sure enough, I had a text and two missed calls from Momma. "I'm sorry, Momma! I guess I still had my phone on silent from work this morning."

"Well, come on and give us all the details!"

I proceeded to fill them in on the whole day's events including why I was out there to begin with, then running into Sam and the discovery of poor Gino. "Macy, have you ever heard Tony mention this Gino guy? Sam was under the impression that Tony was the one that suggested Gino as an investor."

Macy jerked her head up and looked at me wide-eyed. "Tony knows the dead guy? I've never heard him mention anyone named Gino, but he doesn't talk a lot about New York. I know that he was born there, but after high school, he went to live with his grandparents in Italy for a few years so he could go to culinary school."

"When he came back from Italy, where did he live?"

"I think he went back to New York where his parents live. He had his own restaurant for a while, but it got pretty stressful and he needed a change. That's when he decided to try teaching. He applied for the job in Mississippi about five years ago, and you know the rest of the story." She smiled a huge smile that went away as quickly as it appeared, replaced by a worried frown. "He came by this morning to say hello, but I haven't talked to him since then. I went next door after the lunch rush, but everything was locked up tight. I wonder if he's even heard about the murder."

I placed my hand over hers. "Keep trying to call him. I'm sure it would be better for him to hear it from you. I'd hate for him to hear about a friend's death through the town gossip grapevine."

Macy nodded. "I will."

"So, Glory, now that you have a new inside connection with the police department, are you planning on nosing around in this one?" Momma looked up from where she was wiping down the glass display counter. She and Macy exchanged cheeky grins.

"First of all, I have no intention of getting involved in another investigation. One time being knocked in the head and held at gunpoint is enough for me. And second, I do not have a new connection, as you call it. Chief Walker and I aren't even an item."

"When are you going to stop referring to him as Chief, and start calling him Hunt?" Momma asked.

"If—and that's a big if—he ever seems interested enough to ask me out on a real date, I seriously doubt that he would spill any details. I have a feeling he is pretty tight-lipped," I said, immediately regretting my choice of words.

Macy grinned and said, "Maybe so, but wouldn't it be fun trying to loosen them up a little?"

I rolled my eyes, and she and Momma doubled over the display case laughing.

I wiped off the last of the bistro tables and threw the cleaning towel in with the rest of the dirty linens. Pulling the drawstring tight on the laundry bag, I dragged it toward the door. I needed to get home to check on Izzy. It had been a long day, and she'd been cooped up in the house since early this morning. I was sure she would be ready for her supper.

Izzy was my black and white miniature schnauzer. She was a sweetheart, and easily the best dog I'd ever had. Dave and I had gotten her just before he died, and she had been my best friend through those terrible days and months. It's sobering to think how your life can change in a matter of seconds. The fact that Dave was murdered, and the case never solved, continued to nag at the back of my mind no matter how determined I was to move on. The discovery of a drawer full of incriminating evidence convinced me that he had been investigating high profile criminals for tax evasion and illegal accounting practices. Forensic accounting, they called it. Dave's final request was that I take the money he left us and move forward. Coming home to Sweetwater Springs had been the best decision I'd ever made. I knew that it was time for a change and a fresh start, getting back to my roots. Back to a place and people I loved, and I knew loved me. Now that Izzy and I had gotten settled in Alabama and Macy had moved in, I think she had become just as attached to Izzy as I was. It would definitely be hard on all three of us when she eventually moved into her own place.

I gathered my purse and keys, swung the duffle bag full of dirty linens over my shoulder, and headed toward the door.

"I have Rummy Club tonight, so I'll see if they have any juicy information about what's going around town," Momma said. Aside from Bonnie's Cut and Curl, the Rummy Club was the best place in town to get the latest dirt. Those little church ladies could smell drama from miles away.

"Momma, didn't you hear me? I'm not getting involved. Jake and Chief Walker will handle this just fine without us!"

Momma just smiled and waved, as I flipped the sign on the door to CLOSED and walked out.

FIVE

As if on cue, Izzy met me at the door, jumping and wiggling her cute little nub of a tail. I bent down and gave her a rub on the head and then let her out into the fenced backyard while I scooped her food into her dish and got her fresh water. I threw my purse and keys on the kitchen counter and went down the hall to my bedroom. Izzy followed close after and hopped up onto the bed while I changed into some comfy yoga pants and a sweatshirt.

"Well, I'm in the middle of another mess, Izzy." I plopped down on the bed and gathered her into my lap, nuzzling her soft fur. "How do I always end up in the wrong place at the wrong time?" Izzy barked and looked up with those sweet little schnauzer eyes. "Don't look at me like that. I really don't need to get involved in this one, but I can feel that itch coming on." I knew I could tell Izzy and she wouldn't blab to Jake. I just had this thing about making sure that justice was served, and bad people don't get away with murder. "Nope. I'm staying out of this one, Izzy." She jumped off the bed and barked as if to say, "I'll believe it when I see it."

I plodded back into the kitchen and opened the fridge to see what I could scrounge up for supper. My phone signaled an incoming call, and I saw Kelly's face pop up on the screen. I slid my finger across the screen and put her on speaker phone. "Hey, Kelly. Are you on your way?" I yelled in the general direction of the phone with my head still stuck in the refrigerator.

30

"I'm about to leave. I'm gonna drive through and pick up a salad at Moody's. Do you want one?"

"Absolutely! I was just looking for something here but coming up empty. Just grab me a large chef salad. I have some dressings here and plenty of sweet tea."

"Will do! See you in ten."

I wasn't the healthiest eater. I knew I needed to eat more salads, but somehow pizza frequently won that battle. I checked the expiration dates on all the miscellaneous half-empty bottles of salad dressing in the door of the fridge and prayed I found a couple that weren't growing anything fuzzy.

When I heard Kelly's car pull into the driveway, I met her on the porch, holding the door open. Loaded down with salads, purse and laptop bag, she breezed past me and deposited the food on the counter. While I unbagged the food, she pulled out her laptop and opened it up on the kitchen island. I poured us both a glass of iced tea and took a seat next to her. We dug into our salads, and she pulled up the information she had found about Gino Whatshisname.

"I found the list of investors for Pine Bluffs. It's a matter of public record when you file for building permits and things like that. Gino's last name is Moretti. He is from New York City and has made a lot of money through various financial endeavors. It looks like he's really big into real estate. He has his hands in several resorts in upstate New York, as well as in Las Vegas. I also found his name associated with a couple of restaurants. Mostly small places, like family-owned stuff. Nothing major."

"When Sam was telling me about Gino, before we found the body, he mentioned that everyone at the construction offices joked around that he had mob connections. I think it was just because his name is Gino, and he's from New York, but have you seen anything to make you think that might actually be true?" I asked, as I took another bite of salad.

"I haven't had a chance to dig that deep yet. Give me a second and I'll see if I can find anything." Kelly took a drink of tea and typed away on her keyboard while I finished up my salad.

"Well, well, well..." she said. "Looks like our dead friend had a few questionable side businesses to go along with his legit stuff. He, along with two other guys, Bruno Lombardi and Rocco Castillini, were brought up on charges of money laundering and embezzlement. All charges were dropped for lack of evidence." She looked at me and shrugged. "That's all I can find on him."

"Wait!" I said. "Did you say Castillini?"

Macy burst through the door in tears. "Uncle Jake just arrested Tony!" She collapsed on the sofa and sobbed with her face in her hands. Izzy jumped up next to her and whimpered.

"What do you mean he's been arrested? Why in the world would Jake do that?" I asked no one in particular. "Kelly, have you talked to Jake today?"

"Only once, and that was about midafternoon. He just told me not to wait on him for supper."

I turned to a frantic Macy. "Have you talked to Tony?" I asked, already grabbing my cell phone to dial Jake's number.

"No, I never could get him. He never came back to the restaurant, and he never answered my texts or calls, so I drove to his apartment. His car wasn't there."

My phone buzzed in my hand, and I saw the number for the police station. I answered it.

"Glory, this is Hunt. I know you've probably talked to Macy. I wanted to check on her. Jake said she was hysterical when he hung up with her. I just wanted to make sure that she made it home okay."

My heart swelled at the kindness in his voice. "She's here now. She's really upset. Mainly because we have no idea what's going on, and she hasn't been able to talk to Tony all day. Can you tell us anything? What on earth does he have to do with any of this?"

"All I can tell you is that he's being questioned in the murder of Gino Moretti. Please don't ask me to tell you more because I just can't."

"That's just crazy! Tony's a good guy. There's no way he's involved in any of this!" I pleaded. "When can Macy see Tony?"

"Jake is questioning him now, so she can come down in about an hour. Jake should be finished by then."

"We'll be there in an hour." I disconnected the call and looked at Macy and Kelly in disbelief. I sat down beside Macy and wrapped my arms around her, and we all cried.

I knew Macy was crying for Tony, and Kelly was crying for Macy. But I was crying out of frustration. I'd had no intention of getting in the middle of another murder, but here I was again, thrown into the deep end, and I'd be hogtied before I let an innocent guy be convicted for something he didn't do.

FIFTY-EIGHT MINUTES later, all three of us were sitting in the tiny little waiting room at the police station when Jake came out and told Macy he would take her back to see Tony.

Kelly and I settled in and flipped through six-month-old needlework magazines that according to the mailing label, someone named Brenda Hicks had donated. Our only other choice was the Alabama Police Gazette. I was just convincing myself that I needed to learn to cross-stitch when Hunt appeared behind the reception desk.

"Glory, can you come back for a minute?"

"Sure." I eyed Kelly and got up from my chair. I followed him down the hall and into his office. He shut the door behind us, and I immediately broke out in a cold sweat. I wasn't sure if it was the memories of the last time I was here getting fingerprinted and accused of murder, or if it was the woodsy scent of his cologne that was giving me palpitations.

"Am I in trouble again?" I smiled a weak smile and took a seat in the only pitiful little chair in the office.

"No. Not yet, and I'm hoping it's going to stay that way." He looked me straight in the eyes.

"Whatever do you mean, Chief Walker?" I glared back at him and couldn't look away.

"I mean, here we are again. Glory finds a body." He walked around from behind the desk. "Glory swears she isn't going to snoop." He sat on the edge of his desk and leaned back on his hands. "Glory becomes personally involved. Glory gets impatient and feels the need to do my job." He leaned down within inches from my face. "Glory gets herself into trouble." He reached up and brushed my hair out of my eyes and his lips met mine. "Hunt saves Glory from bodily harm, because she doesn't always think before she acts."

I instinctively closed my eyes and melted into the kiss. I opened my eyes and tried to pull away, but he pulled me closer.

"I'm asking you, please don't get involved this time. I know you're concerned for Macy's sake, but let us do our job. If this is what I think it is, it's way more dangerous than it looks." His blue gray eyes locked on mine.

"But you have to know that Tony could never do something like this." I backed up, regaining my composure.

"I'm not saying he did, but we have to do our job. Let us follow the evidence and it will lead us to the killer. And hopefully away from Tony. All I'm asking is that you trust me and try to stay out of trouble. I don't want to have to worry about you. Can you do that?"

"I'll try." It was the best I could do.

SIX

Jake was waiting out in the lobby with Macy and Kelly when I came out. I felt like my face was on fire, and they all looked at me like I was from another planet. I tried not to look anyone in the eye. I felt like a teenager who just got caught in the middle of a good night kiss on the front porch.

"Glory, are you okay? You look flushed. Do you need some water?" Kelly asked.

I shook my head and willed my heartbeat to return to normal. "Macy, you look better. Is Tony okay?" I asked.

"Yes, he's fine. Uncle Jake explained to me that he isn't actually under arrest. They just brought him in for questioning. He has to answer a few more questions, then they will let him go home."

"Good. I'm sure all this will be sorted out soon and they'll know he had nothing to do with this mess."

Macy was still looking at me with that confused look. "Mom, are you sure you're alright? You look like you're about to pass out."

Hunt walked out of his office and motioned for Jake to come in. "You ladies be careful going home, you hear?" He said it to all of us, but his gorgeous eyes were locked on mine and he smiled that smile. The one with the dimple.

Macy and Kelly looked at each other and smiled. Nothing gets by them for long.

"Let's go home." I glared at them and made a beeline for the door.

WHEN WE GOT BACK TO the house, Kelly gathered up her laptop and other items and headed home to an empty house, knowing Jake would be stuck at the station for who knows how long.

Macy and I had just poured glasses of iced tea and collapsed onto the sofa when someone knocked on the door. Macy peeked through the glass and swung the door open. In a rush she wrapped her arms around Tony's neck, and they embraced for a long minute. I got up and poured him a glass of tea and offered him my seat on the sofa next to Macy. I took the chair.

"Tony, I want you to know that none of us believe that you could have anything to do with all this," I said reassuringly. "I have no idea why in the world they would think you did. Just because you suggested Gino as a possible investor for the project?"

"Thank you, but there's more to the story that you should know. I need to be up front with you." He looked at Macy. "Mace, I realize I haven't volunteered a lot of details about my past since we've been dating, and I appreciate the fact that you didn't pressure me for every little detail. Some of it I have tried to put behind me and for good reasons. But now it seems that something, or someone, has come up again and I have to face the things I've tried so hard to forget."

I looked at Macy as she stared at him with tears in her eyes, terrified of what he was about to say.

"It's okay, Tony. Go ahead," I reassured him.

"Gino wasn't just some guy I knew. In fact, Gino contacted Terrance and gave me as a reference. When Terrance called me about him, I told him the truth. That I would not enter into any financial agreement with Gino Moretti. But money talks and Terrance ignored my warnings."

"How do you know Gino?" Macy asked.

"Let me start from the beginning."

Tony began to tell us details of a past that he had tried so desperately to leave behind, and he shared dreams of the life he desperately wanted to build away from all of it.

"Gino Moretti was a friend and business associate of my Uncle Rocco. My uncle, grandfather and entire family were in the 'family business', except for my father. You can call it the mafia or the mob, whatever you want, but he hated it and didn't want any part of it. He kept me away from it as much as he could. When I graduated from high school, he quickly shipped me off to Italy to live with my mom's parents. They owned a restaurant in a small village in Sicily. I enrolled in culinary school nearby and studied for three years before I came back to New York."

I don't know what I expected to hear from Tony, but this was nowhere on my radar. I tried to keep the shocked look off my face as he continued.

"When I returned, I wanted to open my own restaurant. Gino already owned a couple of restaurants and they seemed to be doing well, so I decided to allow him to help finance the venture with the understanding that he was a silent partner and I made all the decisions. He agreed whole-heartedly, and we signed the contract. I didn't know it at the time, but I had just gone into business with the mob."

Tony stopped and took a drink of his tea and shifted in his seat. Macy reached over and placed her hand on his.

"At first the restaurant was doing great. People were flocking to us. We were getting great reviews in all the right publications and blogs. Gino was rarely at the restaurant, but when he was, he just ate dinner and left. Then, about eight months after we opened, I began to see our clientele changing. More nights than not, Gino was there with all his friends and associates. They hung around after hours in the back office. I could see what was happening, but I didn't know how to stop it. After our one-year anniversary celebration, I told Gino that I wanted out. I made the excuse that the restaurant business was just too much pressure and asked if he would be willing to buy out my half of the restaurant. He flat out refused. He knew that my cooking was what made the restaurant a success and that without me, he would lose his shirt. Worse than that, the cover for his criminal activity he'd been working so hard for a year to build would be blown. He would have to start over from the bottom. I talked with my dad and he agreed that I should just cut my losses and get out before I got sucked into the family business. Once you're in, they never let you out. So that's what I did. I lost all the money I had invested in the business, but I saw no way to stay without getting involved. It was worth it all, because it brought me here where I met you, Macy." He held her hands in his and looked into her eyes. "You mean everything to me. I can't lose you."

Tears rolled down Macy's cheeks and he reached up and brushed them away. "Tony, you know I believe in you, and I will stand by you whatever happens. Please believe that."

"I hope you still feel that way when I tell you the rest of the story." He looked at me.

I know I must have looked like a deer in headlights. This was so much to take in, and evidently it wasn't over yet. "So, Tony, when did you find out that Terrance had disregarded your warnings and gone into business with Gino?"

"A few nights ago, I was working late up at the restaurant. Macy had come by and brought me some take out from Moody's."

"Yes, I remember," said Macy. "That was Friday night, right? I remember, because it was so hot and muggy for September, and you had all the doors and windows propped open with the big box fan going."

"Yes. So, after you left, about 8:00, Gino walked in off the street. He told me that he didn't hold it against me that I left him high and dry in New York and that he had a business proposition for me. He said he wanted me to open my restaurant inside the lobby of Pine Bluffs Condominiums."

"I had no idea there were plans for a restaurant out there," I said, taking a drink of my tea.

"Neither did I, and I'm not sure Terrance knew what Gino was planning either. Obviously, I told him I wasn't interested, that I wanted to be in town on Main Street and next door to the bakery. I told him that I had invested all the money I had in buying this place and I had no intention of moving elsewhere. Especially with him."

"Was he upset?" Macy asked.

"You could say that. He started screaming. I could see a crowd gathering outside on the sidewalk and people peering through the window. He said if I didn't agree to move my restaurant to the Bluffs, he would open one of his own and bring in the best Italian chefs in New York City to put me out of business. I knew he had enough money to make good on that promise. I was seething with anger, and before I realized what I was doing I had picked up a hammer and chased him out the door." Tony put his head in his hands.

"So those witnesses are the reason you are a suspect now that Gino has turned up dead." It made more sense now. I could see why Jake had to bring him in. From the outside looking in, it looked really bad for Tony. I just hoped Jake and Hunt didn't settle for the easy way out.

I looked sympathetically over at Tony. "I know it's been a long day and you've already been through this once, but could you tell me what questions Jake asked?"

"Sure. I'll be glad to stay here all night if it will help convince you that I'm innocent and that I need your help to get the police to see that." He took a deep breath, exhaled and continued. "He asked me for my alibi. He wanted to know where I was all day and account for my movements."

I retrieved my notebook and pen from the kitchen counter and settled in to take notes.

SEVEN

"Okay, let's start from the beginning. Tell me everything you did after you saw Macy and Momma early this morning."

Macy tapped her fingers on the table. "I remember, it was about 8:30 when you stopped by to say good morning. I know, because I had set the oven timer for the dark chocolate pound cakes for 8:25 and I had just taken them out and was placing them on the cooling racks."

"Okay, there's the first marker on our timeline. What next?" I was desperately praying that he would remember something that would unquestionably give him an airtight alibi that we could share with Jake, and the police could move on to another suspect.

"After I visited for a few minutes, I went back next door and worked on the menu for the restaurant. I was browsing on-line to get ideas for the menu."

"You mean looking up recipes?" I asked, totally surprised and a little confused, thinking he would be stealing recipes off the internet and passing them off as his own.

"No, of course not! All my recipes are my own or a family recipe handed down from my grandmother in Italy. No, I mean menu design ideas. Like artwork and layout."

"Oh! Right!" I said and blew out a breath of relief.

"I have some ideas, but I'm not a great artist, so I searched for graphic designers in the area, and one of the search results was a guy in Baileyville, Alabama. The phone number listed on the website must have been outdated, because when I tried to call, it was disconnected.

Baileyville was a community about an hour north of Sweetwater Springs. It had its own Post Office, so I guess technically it would be considered a town, but it was even smaller than Sweetwater Springs and farther into the county. Tony would have had to drive through the forest on County Road 125 right past the turn off for Pine Bluffs.

"I dropped the address into my computer. It wasn't that far away, so on a whim, I decided to take a chance and drive over to see if he was available to talk."

Excited, I sat up straighter, "So this guy can verify your alibi!"

Tony shook his head, and my excitement took a nosedive. "Well, not exactly. After I drove all the way over there, the place was closed on Mondays. Locked up tight, so I never got to talk to him."

I glanced over at Macy. She was looking more and more distressed.

She looked at Tony, "What I don't understand is why you didn't return any of my texts or calls."

He gave her a sheepish look. "I'm so sorry, Mace. I guess I had been so intent on finding this designer guy, that I walked right out of the restaurant without my phone. I just scribbled down the address, grabbed my laptop and took off out the door. When I got just past the north end of the lake, I realized I had left it, but it was too late to turn around. I didn't see your missed texts and calls until I got back to the restaurant. I had just gotten back when the police walked in," he said squeezing her hand.

"Did anyone see you in Baileyville? Did you speak to anyone?" I asked hopefully.

"I doubt it. I only stopped once, and that was to grab a cup of coffee at a little roadside café."

"Do you have the receipt?"

Again, he shook his head glumly, "No, I paid cash and told the cashier I didn't need the receipt. I doubt she would even remember me; she barely even looked up from the register."

"What time did you stop at the café?"

"I think it was about 10:30. I remember thinking it was still a little early for lunch, so I just went with the coffee."

This was not looking good so far. "So just so I have the timeline straight, you left your restaurant a little after 9:00 and drove to Baileyville. That's a little over an hour. You arrived at the designer's closed office about 10:15. You headed back and stopped for coffee before you left Baileyville at about 10:30," I said, making sure I got as many details on the timeline as possible.

Tony nodded, continuing to wring his hands in worry.

"So, if that's the case, shouldn't that have put you back in Sweetwater Springs no later than 11:30?"

Something wasn't lining up. There was a big gap in Tony's timeline, and suddenly I felt sick to my stomach. "You said that you had just returned when the police walked in. I didn't discover the body until a little after noon, so the officers wouldn't have even known about the murder yet. Jake called Macy on her way home from the bakery just after 3:00 to tell her that you had been taken down to the station. Where did you go between 11:30 and 3:00?"

A look of realization crossed Tony's face when it registered that he truly had no alibi at all. He dropped his head into his hands and let out an exhausted breath. He raised his head and looked at Macy, "I didn't want to worry you about all of this. I have been so stressed since Gino showed up the other night because I knew it meant trouble. He is nothing but bad news, and I didn't want anything to do with him or his restaurant. With all the remodeling and construction noise in the restaurant, I needed some time alone in the quiet. I just needed to think and pray and gather my thoughts. On my way back from Baileyville, when I reached the north end of the lake, I turned off and found a quiet spot to just sit. Since I didn't have my phone, I guess the time just got away from me and I ended up staying longer than I realized. By the time I got back to town, it was almost 3:00."

Tony looked at both of us. I guess he saw a flash of doubt in my eyes because he began to panic.

"You have to believe me! Macy has told me how you have solved murders and helped the police. Please say that you will help me."

My heart really did hurt for him, but my biggest concern was Macy. I didn't want her to get hurt, and I certainly didn't want her mixed up with a killer or the mob. But, after taking one look at her eyes begging me to help Tony, I agreed.

"Okay, I'll do what I can. I will ask around and see if I can find out how seriously they are looking at other suspects. In the meantime, cooperate with Jake and the police department and if you remember anything that might help us confirm your alibi, let me know. It's been a long day for all of us. Go home and get some rest. Why don't you come by the bakery first thing tomorrow and we'll come up with a plan?"

Tony nodded and thanked me as he got up to leave.

After Macy walked him out to his car, she closed the door behind her and looked at me with tears in her eyes. "Mom, you do believe him, don't you?"

"I want to. I really do. I like Tony and I know you do too, but I realized tonight how much we don't know about him."

"Mom, I don't just like him, I'm in love with him. Even though I don't know everything about him, I really believe that I know him. He could never do something like this."

"I promise I will do my best to give him the benefit of the doubt and try not to jump to conclusions."

As I lay in bed staring at the ceiling, a million thoughts scrambled for my attention. Earlier this evening when Kelly read off the list of previous charges against Gino, I couldn't help but think about the last time I heard those terms, money laundering, tax evasion, illegal accounting practices. My mind kept going back to Dave's death and the ominous envelopes I had safely hidden away in a safe deposit box at the bank. When Rocco Castillini's name was listed as a defendant in the same case, I wondered if Dave had ever investigated Tony's family. That was something I was not sure I was ready to find out. I wanted to trust that Tony was telling us the truth, but it all sounded too convenient. My first priority was Macy.

I prayed for calm and peace for Tony and Macy, and I prayed for wisdom and direction for Jake and Hunt. The best way to get them to stop looking at Tony was to give them other suspects to focus on. And that's what I intended to do.

EIGHT

I had finally fallen asleep around 2:00, but tossed and turned most of the night, revisiting the murder site in my head over and over. The bakery opened at 7:00 each morning, so that meant rise and shine on the days I helped Macy. I heard noises in the kitchen and knew that Macy was already up and making coffee. I flung back the covers and with one fell swoop, swung my legs over the side of the bed and sat up. Some days that's the only way to start the day. Take a deep breath and dive in. I slipped my feet into my pink flamingo slippers and headed to the kitchen, my slippers making a swishing sound as I shuffled down the hall.

Macy was sitting at the kitchen table with a cup of coffee in front of her and staring intently at her phone. I grabbed a mug and poured myself a cup, breathing in the dark roast scent. I let Izzy out into the backyard and pulled out a chair next to Macy.

She looked up at me and smiled. "Mom, I was just reading my morning devotion on my Bible app, and you'll never believe what it was about this morning."

I scooted over next to her so I could see the screen also.

"It's about how we can trust God to deliver us from false accusations." I listened as Macy read the verse aloud.

"In my distress I called to the Lord, and He answered me. Deliver me, O Lord, from lying lips, from a deceitful tongue. What shall be given to you, and what more shall be done to you, you de-

ceitful tongue? A warrior's sharp arrows with glowing coals will be your reward." Psalm 120:1-4

I smiled. "Yes, God is still in charge, even when we think things are spinning out of control. We can trust Him." I took her hand and we prayed together that God would protect Tony and deliver him from those who are trying to accuse him of something he didn't do, and that Jake and Hunt would be able to bring the real killer to justice soon.

Izzy scratched at the back door, letting us know she was ready to come back in. Macy let her in and fed her while I grabbed a quick shower. We had several things to do today that I was hoping would shed some light on other suspects, but first we had a bakery to open.

Macy unlocked the door and punched the code into the security alarm. It was early, barely daylight, but such is the life of a baker, as I was quickly learning. I flipped the light switch and the massive, classic chandelier Macy had chosen hung from the vaulted ceiling in the center of the room and illuminated the beautiful space. She and Tony had done such a great job with the renovation and design of the place. It had always been my favorite storefront on Main Street, even when I was a little girl. Originally a furniture store, its impressive, Gone with the Wind-style staircase took your breath away as you entered the doors. The original hardwood floors had been refinished, and Macy had worked so hard pulling down paneling to expose the beautiful brick walls. A large glass case of baked goods and coffee shop area were located to the left as you entered, with tables and chairs to the right of the staircase. Upstairs, the open loft surrounded and overlooked the entire first floor. It displayed an assortment of kitchen décor and items, including cookbooks, tea towels, coffee mugs and much more.

We both tied our aprons around our waists and got to work. Macy started a batch of raspberry scones, which would be her pastry special today. I pulled out a couple of quiches and the usual assortment of muffins that she had made in advance and kept in the walk-in cooler. She slipped two pans of scones and the quiches into the oven and set the timer, and we walked thru the swinging door from the kitchen. We were both startled to find Tony standing at the counter. He looked worse than he had the night before and I doubted he got any more sleep than either of us did.

"Good morning!" I said, trying to exude more energy in my voice than I felt. "I didn't hear the bell over the door jingle! You startled us!" I laughed. "Did you get any sleep last night?"

"Not a lot." He leaned on the counter. "I couldn't turn off my brain. All the worst-case scenarios kept popping into my mind."

"What we all need is a good dose of caffeine while we sit for a minute and put our heads together."

Macy poured herself and Tony an espresso while I got my usual large iced coffee with sugar free vanilla. I had only been on the coffee-train for a few months and I was still a newbie. I was learning all the different nuances of the coffee world, but it was still hard for me to drink a lot of the hot stuff in warm weather. With everything set to open, we had about a half an hour to talk through things and come up with a list of possible suspects to give Jake and Hunt somewhere else to focus the investigation.

"Our first question would obviously be, who would want Gino dead? Since Macy and I don't know a lot about him personally, maybe you can give us more insight on that." I looked over at Tony, pencil at the ready.

"Well, I would start with the family." Tony glanced up at Macy for a split second, then continued to stare at his coffee cup as if it was going to manifest the name of the killer written in the swirls of cream on top. "I talked to my dad last night. Like I said, he doesn't really have much contact with the rest of the family any longer, but he said that he would call his sister, my Aunt Celia, and see if she had heard anything. She still goes to Sunday lunch at my grandparents' house after mass most weeks."

"Mass? I hadn't thought about your family being Catholic, but I guess it makes sense, being Italian." I stopped short. "I'm sorry, that sounded like a very stereotypical thing to say."

"It's fine. I was raised Catholic. It wasn't until I moved to Mississippi, and Macy invited me to church with her, that I started attending a Baptist church. It's definitely different, but I do like it." He smiled.

"Okay, so maybe you'll hear from your dad soon after he talks to your aunt. Let's look at this from a different angle. Maybe it wasn't Gino, personally, they were targeting. Maybe someone is just trying to derail the resort development."

Tony nodded. "Maybe someone felt like the best way to stop the construction is to cut off the money supply. Gino was the major investor. Without him, it will struggle to continue."

"I think we should put some of the lake landowners on the list. Maybe Chris Lester or Jeff Newsome. I overheard their wives talking in here yesterday morning about how their property values were taking a hit already. Megan Lester said something to the effect that she didn't think they'd have to worry about that problem much longer. Maybe she knew her husband was going to take care of the problem."

"I agree," Macy said. "Wasn't she the one spouting off veiled threats toward Terrance at the Ladies' Club Meeting a few months ago?"

"Yes, she said he'd better 'watch his back.'" I wrote down Chris Lester and Jeff Newsome. "Chris owns the newspaper, and there have been some pretty biased articles published lately about the resort. I don't think I've read one positive thing since it started."

Macy shook her head sadly. "I just can't see how someone could take a person's life over something like property values. It's only money."

"One of the comments that Cindy Newsome made to me yesterday makes me think differently. She said business comes before anything else at their house. And business means money."

The timer for the scones and quiches buzzed in the kitchen. That was our cue to get up and start the business day. I walked over and turned the sign to OPEN and tucked my notebook away behind the counter. While Macy pulled the scones out of the oven and arranged them on a glass pedestal cake stand, I changed the chalkboard sign to announce the day's pastries and the quiches available. The Quiche Lorraine smelled amazing, but my favorite was the Caprese Quiche. The aroma of mozzarella, Roma tomatoes and fresh basil caused my stomach to remind me in no uncertain terms that it was time for breakfast. I took one last look around and made sure everything in the display case was in good order. Tony gathered up our trash and, after cleaning off the table, gave Macy a sweet peck on the cheek and left for the restaurant next door.

NINE

The door jingled and we both looked up with a smile when Momma sauntered in.

"What are you doing here today?" I asked. "This is my day to work."

"I've got a hair appointment at Bonnie's in a bit, so I thought I'd swing by here and give you the lowdown on all the dirt that was dished last night at Rummy Club." She smiled mischievously.

"Do tell!" I raised one eyebrow.

"It seems that the hot topic of conversation was definitely the unfortunate Mr. Moretti. There were several theories of who put the hole in his forehead, but one in particular grabbed my attention." Momma poured herself a large decaf coffee with a little splash of almond milk.

"Keep going," I urged.

"Well, Martha Jean said that she heard from Josie Johnson that Gino had been staying at the Lakeside for the last week. I'm supposing while he was here checking on the progress of his investment and meeting with Terrance."

Josie Johnson and her husband owned and operated the Lakeside Motel, the only lodging establishment within thirty miles of Sweetwater Springs. "That can't be much of a revelation since that's the only motel in town." I rolled my eyes.

"I'm not finished." Momma huffed, and I nodded for her to go on. "Two days ago, another car showed up with New York plates. Josie said that she never saw who it belonged to, but whoever it was, has been staying in the room with Gino."

My eyes widened. "And she has no idea who? Does she know if it's a man or a woman?"

"She said that they hung the Do Not Disturb sign on the door and the other car rarely left the parking lot, so she never felt like she had a good chance to sneak a peek. She did catch a whiff of what she described as 'high dollar toilet water.'"

"So, it sounds like it's probably a woman! Does he have a wife or a girlfriend?" I wondered out loud. Maybe that was something Tony could tell us.

"If it is a woman, why on earth wouldn't she just come down with him? That's a very long drive for a woman alone from New York to Alabama," Macy commented. She looked up as the door jingled and an older couple came in and perused the delectable pastry options. She slipped over to help them, and Momma left for Bonnie's.

A fairly steady stream of customers continued throughout the morning. Even though Macy had only been open a few weeks, it seemed she already had a group of "regulars" who had found a home at Macy's on Main. The four retirees sat around a table in the far corner each with a cup of coffee, sharing a basket of assorted muffins. They had just pulled out a container of dominoes. I could hear the men laughing at each other's tall tales. I recognized a couple of them from church, Jimmy Don Baker and Billy Franks. A third one was Leo Dixon, the husband of Bonnie June, who was at this moment doing who-knows-what to Momma's hair and I hoped giving her some juicy gossip we could use. The fourth man I recognized as a retired attorney in town who also served on the city council.

His name was Otto Becker. Over the clatter of dominoes on the table, I heard someone mention the ruckus at the latest city council meeting. I picked up a carafe of coffee and sidled over to see if they needed refills.

"Chris Lester threatened he'd do what?" I heard Leo ask.

"He said he had done some digging and he had a story that was gonna shut down Terrance and the project for good. Said he won't stand by and watch his property value take a nosedive while Terrance brings in rental riff raff." Otto leaned his chair back on two legs. "Lester said the resort should be built on the commercial end of the lake and he was gonna keep on fighting it until Terrance lost every penny he and all his investors have put into it."

"More coffee, anyone?" They all nodded and held their cups up in my direction.

"That little girl of yours sure has herself a nice little place here, Glory," Billy commented and they all heartily agreed.

"Thank you. I'm pretty proud of her. I think the new resort is really gonna be the boost our town needs, and I have a feeling the tourists will start pouring in." I watched their faces for any kind of reaction.

"I have to agree with you. But after what happened out there yesterday, I just hope it isn't dead in the water. No pun intended." Billy said sheepishly.

Otto nodded and looked up at me. "I heard you were the one who found the guy. I'm sorry you had to go through that again. Didn't you find the body in the cemetery a few months back?"

I nodded.

"And the one at the old Baylor place?" Billy added.

I nodded again. "It seems I have a knack for being in the wrong place at the wrong time." I let out a nervous laugh. "I couldn't help but overhear about the city council meeting. Any idea what the big scoop is that Chris Lester is planning to print?"

"I heard it was something to do with the guy who got killed, so I don't know if he'll still run it or not. After the meeting was over, I heard him telling Jeff Newsome that he was supposed to be meeting someone to get the last bit of proof before he ran it."

"Hmm... any idea who he was meeting?"

"No, sorry. He didn't say. But whoever it was, the meeting would have to have been yesterday or today because the deadline is at 5:00 today since they go to print tonight."

I topped off all their cups and let them get back to their dominoes game. I was just about to fill Macy in on what the men had told me when the door jingled again and in walked Hunt.

"Mornin' ladies." He said, waltzing through the door.

"Well, if it isn't Sweetwater's finest," I said, trying my best not to meet Hunt's gaze and immediately regretting my choice of words. Not that he wasn't fine. He definitely was, but I didn't want it to go to his handsome head. After everything that had happened since our visit to the police station last night, I had almost forgotten about the incident in his office. I had deliberately pushed it to the back of my mind, concentrating on Tony and the murder investigation. But it came barreling back to the front of my brain like a '66 Mustang with no brakes. I was desperately stomping the floorboard, but nothing was stopping it.

Suddenly, I felt lightheaded and the back of my neck broke out in a cold sweat.

"Mom, are you okay? Do you need to sit down?" Macy asked, obviously concerned at my lack of color.

"Nope. I'm fine," I lied. "Just had a little too much caffeine this morning."

"It's almost lunchtime. Why don't you go grab some solid food? I'll be fine here for a little while," Macy suggested.

"I was just about to get a sandwich at Moody's. I came by to see if you'd like to join me." Hunt shifted from one foot to the other and smiled. Dang those dimples.

My legs went all jellified and I managed a nod. As I grabbed my purse from behind the counter, my notepad fell to the floor. Hunt watched as I hurriedly stuffed it in my purse. He grinned and lifted an eyebrow but didn't comment.

"Shall we?" He motioned toward the door like a game show host showing the grand prize behind curtain number two.

TEN

Moody's was pretty busy for mid-day on a Tuesday. We placed our orders and found a table near the window.

"Feeling better now?" he asked as I took a big bite of the burger the server had just dropped off.

"Much. Three cups of coffee and no solid food for breakfast must not agree with me."

"How's Macy doing? Was she able to talk to Tony after we let him go home last night?"

"Yes, he came by the house on his way back to his apartment. She's okay. We're both confident that he's innocent and are depending on you and Jake to stop wasting your time looking at Tony and concentrate on other suspects."

He frowned and reached across the table and took my hand. "Glory, I said it last night and I'll say it again. We have to follow the evidence. When it leads us away from Tony, that's where we'll go. In the meantime, put your little suspect notebook away and trust us to do our jobs."

I felt my cheeks flush. "You saw that, huh?"

"Of course, I did. I'm a detective. Nothing gets by me." He grinned.

"Well, Detective Walker, how's the detecting going? Have you found a murder weapon yet? What about time of death?"

"Whoa, slow down, Sherlock. You know I can't discuss the investigation with you."

I took a drink of my iced tea. "Can't blame a girl for trying." I shrugged.

"How about we just enjoy our lunch and change the subject. Why don't you tell me a little about yourself?"

"Not much to tell. Grew up here. Moved away for thirty years. Now I'm back. Now, tell me about yourself."

Hunt rolled his eyes. "Can we elaborate a little more, maybe? Tell me about your husband. Where did y'all meet? Where did you live in Texas? You know, I'm from there."

I wasn't sure I wanted to tell Hunt the whole complicated story of Dave and his secret life, but I took a deep breath and decided to give him the Cliffs Notes version. "Dave and I met in high school here in Sweetwater Springs. We got married and moved to Texas when he got a job with an accounting firm there. Macy was born there. It was a great life until the end, and then it wasn't."

"What do you mean, until the end?"

"He was murdered, and his killer was never found. The case went cold and I gave up trying to convince the government to keep it open."

"What do you mean, the government? I thought he was just an accountant."

Suddenly, Hunt's eyes went wide. "What did you say your husband's name was?"

"Dave Harper. Why?"

Staring into space he began, "He was working undercover. It was assumed, but never proven that it was a mob hit, right?"

I couldn't believe what I was hearing. "How do you know that?" I sat up and pushed back from the table.

"I was one of the detectives assigned to the case. When the government shut down the investigation, I still had questions. I was told in no uncertain terms to back off."

I could feel my heart pounding as he talked.

"When I refused," he continued, "I was given the option of being put on permanent leave or being transferred."

"Did you follow me here?" I asked in a panic, almost screaming the word "follow."

"No! I had no idea you were from here. One of the guys on the force had vacationed here on the lake with his family for years and when he saw this job on the list, he suggested I grab it. I swear I had no idea. Please believe me, Glory. I would never deceive you like that." He took my hand and held tight as I tried to pull it away. I needed to have air. I couldn't breathe, but this time it was for a totally different reason.

"Please take me back to the bakery." The tears rolled down my cheeks.

"Of course. Can we talk about this more, later? I need you to understand," he pleaded. "When this case is closed, we can talk about it, okay?"

I nodded, still feeling numb. Like two worlds had just collided and everything was spiraling out of control. Out of control— I was immediately reminded of the Bible verses Macy and I read this morning and how I encouraged her to trust. My exact words were, "God is still in charge even when we think things are spinning out of control." I guess it was time for me to walk my talk.

Hunt dropped me off at the bakery and I thanked him and went in without another word.

Macy was in the kitchen baking for tomorrow. She stuck her head out of the swinging door when she heard the door jingle.

"Are you feeling better? You still don't look so good. Are you sick or is it something else?"

She knew me too well. She could always tell when I had something on my mind.

"I'm fine, honey. Really, I am. I just have a lot on my mind. I feel so bad for Tony and I want to help get this resolved for both of your sakes."

She nodded. "I understand. I feel the same way and I want to do anything I can to help him."

"Will you be okay here by yourself until closing?"

"Sure, Mom. It's almost 1:00 now and I'll close up at 3:00. I can handle a couple of hours."

"I have a couple of leads I want to follow up on before I head home. What are your plans tonight?"

"Tony said he'd be finished at the restaurant by around 3:00, so we planned to grab an early supper and he can bring me home."

"That's perfect. After the crazy couple of days we've had, a quiet evening at home is just what I need to think through some things. I'll talk to you later tonight." I dug around in my purse and found my keys and headed to my car.

I unlocked the door and tossed my purse across to the passenger seat and started to get in the car when I saw the trash bag full of purses in my back seat. I had forgotten all about them. I'd need to take them into the house when I got home later. But first, I wanted to find out more about who was staying at the Lakeside Motel with Gino.

I pulled into the parking lot and parked in front of the motel office where I could see Josie folding clean towels.

"Afternoon, Glory! What brings you out our way?"

"Momma heard something at Rummy Club last night about Gino Moretti having a visitor." I glanced across the parking lot to a black Lexus SUV with out of state tags. "Anything you can tell me about it? Have you seen anyone?"

"You know it's strange that someone would go to all the trouble to stay out of sight, but not try to hide their car. I'm not sure who it is, but I'm pretty sure it's a woman—either that or it's a sweet smellin' man." Josie waggled her eyebrows.

"Do you mind if I take a stroll over that way and look around?"

"Be my guest. I've been doing laundry all morning, so I can't say if they've been in or out today. Mr. Moretti paid for two weeks in advance, so I got no problem with them till the money runs out. When it does, I'll make sure they hit the road quick enough."

"Thanks, Josie," I said as I strode across the lot. The SUV engine was popping and crackling like it had just been driven and was still cooling down. I laid my hand on the hood and it still felt warm.

"What are you doing to my car?" I jerked my hand away and spun around. A voluptuous blonde in a white tank top with big hot pink lips on the front, skintight black jeans and six-inch heels was standing in the doorway of Gino's room holding a handgun pointed right at my face.

"Oh, I'm so sorry! I was just admiring your car." I slowly moved my hand away from the vehicle and tried to sound calm. "I just love the look of a Lexus, don't you?"

"Well obviously, since I own one." Touché.

She lowered the gun, and I let out the breath I was holding.

"My name's Glory, what's yours?" I stuck my hand out like I was used to people pointing guns at me all day long.

"Bianca Moretti." She ignored my outstretched hand.

"Oh, you must be Gino's wife. I'm really sorry for your loss."

She nodded. "How do you know Gino?" she asked suspiciously.

"I actually never got to meet him. I was the one who found him after the—unfortunate incident."

Her shoulders dropped, and she lowered her head and stared at the ground. "He was excited about this job. He had big plans for this resort," she sighed.

There were a couple of chairs outside each motel room. I motioned to them. "Can we sit for a minute? I'd like to ask you a few questions."

"Sure. I just got back from the morgue. The cops called me to identify his body."

"When did you get into town?" I knew the answer, but I wanted to see if she would own up to the fact that she got here before the murder.

"I just got in this morning. Drove straight through the night from New York and went straight to the station before I came here to gather his things."

"Bless your heart. You must be so tired," I said, as she put her hand to her mouth to stifle a very fake yawn.

"Yes, I'm exhausted. I really do need to rest before the long drive back."

"I understand. How long had you and Gino been married?"

"Ten wonderful years. We were so happy. He doted on me, you know. Bought me anything I wanted. Paid for trips all over the world for me and my girlfriends. I'm going to miss him so much."

I coughed, trying to stifle a chuckle. "Well, I'll let you get some rest. How long before you head back up north?"

"I'll have to wait until they release his body, but that handsome detective said it could be soon. I guess they must have a pretty good suspect."

I wondered which handsome detective she was referring to. The twinge of something in my stomach made me realize that I hoped it had better be Jake.

On the drive back to town, I tried to sort the truth from the lies in my conversation with Mrs. Moretti. I knew she had been there for several days. I also knew that she owned a handgun since I had seen it up close and personal. She didn't seem to be the least bit sincere about losing her husband. I got the distinct impression that she was gonna miss Gino's money much more than she was gonna miss poor Gino. But, why would she want to kill him? I was putting her on the list, but I still had to find her motive.

ELEVEN

It was almost 2:30 and I still had plenty of time to stop by the Sweetwater Herald and see what I could find out about the article Chris Lester had been working on. I found an empty parking spot just in front of the newspaper office. I doubted if anyone would be forthcoming about the information in the article, but it was worth a shot. I grabbed my purse and slung it over my shoulder. As I turned to close the car door, I caught a glimpse again of the bag of purses in the back seat. That's it! That's the perfect excuse for my visit to the office. I would ask them to do a short community support article about the Ladies' Club Purse Auction. The money raised this year was going to help buy new playground equipment for the elementary school.

The newspaper office was located in a small stand-alone building that was just off the town square across from the courthouse. The old stone building was one of many in town listed on the Historic Register or so read the plaque to the right of the glass doors. I swung open the door and entered into a beehive of activity. It was one big open room with several metal desks spaced all over. The noise of phones ringing and keyboards clicking was deafening. But not one person looked my way. I might as well have been invisible. After the third person walked right past me with a cell phone glued to their ear, a young girl headed toward an empty desk with a fresh cup of coffee spotted me and walked over.

"Can I help you?" she asked in a slightly annoyed tone of voice.

"Is it always this busy here?" I asked incredulously.

"Only on print day. Is there something I can do for you?" she asked again, no mistaking the annoyance this time.

"My name is Glory Harper. I was hoping I could speak to someone about writing an article about the upcoming Ladies' Club Purse Auction to raise money for the elementary school playground upgrade."

"Hmm, well, we do like to support community causes, so let me see if Mr. Lester has time to speak with you. I know he was looking for a last-minute filler for an article we had to pull from tomorrow's edition. Have a seat and I'll ask him." She directed me to a metal chair near the door, so I sat. But I jumped right back to my feet when Chris Lester appeared in the doorway of what looked to be the only private office in sight.

"Mrs. Harper, you have information about the fundraiser?" We shook hands. "Come this way, it's quieter in here." He motioned for me to follow him into his office. "I'm surprised that my wife, Megan, hasn't mentioned this to me before now. Her being the president, and all."

"The young woman who was in charge of the auction this year had to step down unexpectedly and I was asked to take over, so I assumed she would want me to cover the publicity and promotion also." I had no idea if that was part of my job, but it sounded good anyway. "Here is a copy of the flyer we designed for this year's auction." I pulled one out of my purse and handed it to him. "I think it has all the pertinent information."

He proceeded to ask a few questions and got a couple of quotes for the article. "I'm glad you came by when you did."

"Oh, why is that?"

"I'm sure you noticed the chaos going on in the workroom. That's because we've been scrambling for something to fill the spot of an article we won't be able to run. There aren't that many newsworthy happenings around here, so it's not always easy to find enough news to fill up the paper."

"You'd think with the murder and all, that you'd have a front-page story to die for!" I laughed at my own pun, but he didn't even crack a smile. I was hoping he would feel free to expound on his investigative prowess and tell me more.

"True. I had a story that was going to blow the whole resort project out of the water, but after that guy went and got himself whacked by the mob, the police put a gag order on me. I can't run any of the information I had ready until they give me the go ahead. They say it might tip off the killer and derail their investigation."

"What on earth makes you think it was the mob? Do we have mob connections around here I don't know about?" I asked, feigning ignorance. "What do you know about the man that was killed?"

Lester puffed out his chest. "I have information that will stir up enough of a stink that Terrance Wolfe will never be able to finish that monstrosity. That Gino guy was as connected as they come. I can't say any more. If that detective gets wind that I told you this much, he may not allow me to print anything. Sooner or later, I'm gonna be able to tweak the same story. It's just that now, it will be good riddance to bad rubbish, an obituary of sorts," he said with an ugly sneer on his face.

"Mr. Lester, it's no secret that you and other lake landowners are dead set against that development. How will the readers know that you aren't just concocting some hairbrained story to stop the construction? Do you have any proof?"

He shifted in his chair, and I could have sworn his hand moved slowly toward his desk drawer, but then stopped. "Mr. Moretti himself had agreed to meet with me so I could ask him the facts face to face, but he never showed."

"When was this meeting supposed to take place?"

"He said if I would meet him at the motel yesterday morning at 10:00, he'd let me ask anything I wanted."

"And you went to the motel?"

"Yes. I knocked several times and waited around. His car was there, but he never came to the door.

"His red sports car was there?"

"No, I didn't see a sports car. I just saw a Lexus SUV. It had New York plates, so I just assumed it was his."

I wondered if Chris Lester could be that devious? Could he have killed Gino and driven him out to the site in his own car to dump him, then left his car there to make the police think Gino was killed at the scene?

"Mr. Lester, do you know how to drive a manual transmission?"

This time there was no mistaking when his hand moved all the way over to the drawer and he opened it, pretending to be searching for something. I'm sure it was for my benefit, because he watched my eyes land on the handgun inside. "Mrs. Harper, surely you aren't accusing me of murder?"

"Not at all. I was just curious. You know so many people these days have never learned to drive a stick shift. I guess it's becoming sort of a lost art." I rose to my feet. "I need to be go-

ing now. Thank you again for agreeing to promote the auction."
I turned and got out of there as fast as I could.

I sank into the driver's seat of my car and took a deep
breath. I threw it into gear and tried to hold my emotions in
check until I got home. I parked the car and headed into the
house. Izzy met me at the door ready for her supper and a potty
break. I put some food and water in her dishes and poured myself a glass of sweet tea. When she finished her food, I decided a
walk around the block would be good for both of us. I snapped
her leash to her collar, and we headed out. The crisp, fresh air
was just what I needed to clear my head. We walked past house
after house.

"Izzy, why would Chris Lester practically threaten me with
a gun if he isn't guilty? If he went to the motel like he claims
and Gino wasn't there, he could have just gone to the construction site to find him. If Lester is lying and Gino was there, he
could've killed him at the motel and then driven him out to the
site in Gino's car. I'm sure he could've just gotten an Uber back
to the motel to get his car." Izzy stopped every ten feet to sniff
and see which of the neighborhood dogs had been there last.
I'm not sure she was listening to me, but I kept talking. "And
what do you make of Bianca? She seems a little high mainte-
nance. I wonder if Gino was happy to get a break from her for a
while." I grabbed the mail out of the mailbox and headed back
into the house.

It had been an emotionally stressful day and I felt like I
was about to collapse, both body and mind. I longed to just
be. Not think about anything. Just be. I picked up my phone
and scrolled to the music app and connected to the Bluetooth
speaker system Macy had given me for my birthday. I selected

Rat Pack Radio, sat back on the sofa and closed my eyes as Frank Sinatra crooned a soft melody. It was my guilty pleasure. I think I must have been born in the wrong decade. Nothing relaxed me more than old classics from an era gone by.

Unfortunately, my peaceful state of mind didn't last long, because my lunch discussion with Hunt kept creeping into my head. I didn't want to think about it, but I knew I needed to hear him out. Now that the shock had worn off, I should probably apologize for going all ballistic in the middle of Moody's. As I closed my eyes and took a deep breath, a Bible verse kept coming to my mind: *"He will keep you in perfect peace, who's mind is stayed on Him."* That's the peace I needed in the middle of everything that had happened lately.

A knock at the door roused me from my ten seconds of peace and calm. Kelly let herself in and rushed over to sit beside me on the sofa.

"Oh, Glory! Hunt told Jake about your discussion over lunch. Are you okay? Jake said that Hunt is so worried about you." She put her arm around my shoulder. That must have been all the encouragement I needed to totally lose it and fall apart. I sobbed as Kelly patted and rubbed my shoulder. When I regained my composure, I looked at her.

"I'm sorry I'm such a blubbering hot mess." We both laughed uncontrollably out of exhaustion. I don't even know what we were laughing about but it was something I needed desperately. "I've not only been trying to solve a murder, but I've also been threatened with a gun—twice today—and found out that the guy I'm crazy about may or may not have followed me here like a stalker from my past life that I've tried to get away from."

"Well, at least one good thing has come from it." Kelly grinned.

"Pray tell, what could that be?" I straightened up on the sofa and looked at her.

"At least you finally admitted that you're crazy about Hunt, because he's sure crazy about you. You really need to talk to him and let him explain his involvement in Dave's investigation."

"I know. And I will. But it's going to have to wait. He needs to focus on the murder investigation, and we need to clear Tony's name. Then I can think about that."

Kelly agreed. She got up and poured herself a glass of iced tea while I pulled out my trusty notebook and the three of us—me, Kelly and Frank Sinatra—got to work.

TWELVE

After I had filled Kelly in on all that had transpired to-day—the conversation with the men at the bakery, the visit to Bianca Moretti and my little meeting with Chris Lester—we updated our suspect list.

"We already have Chris Lester on the list, but I think he moves to the top as number one suspect. We know he owns a handgun. He had an appointment to meet Gino the morning of the murder. Maybe he went to the motel and when Gino didn't answer the door, he drove to the resort. They fought and he shot Gino in the office trailer and dragged his body out to the site."

Kelly nodded as I wrote. "Maybe when he threatened to reveal Gino's shady past in the newspaper, Gino went after him and he killed Gino in self-defense."

"I suppose that's plausible." I continued to jot down the second possible scenario. "Do we know a time of death yet? I wish I could get Hunt or Jake to throw me a bone and at least tell me that much."

"We definitely need to add the wife to the list." Kelly took a big drink of her tea.

"She certainly had every opportunity, but I just don't see a good motive, yet. He seems to be worth more to her alive than dead." I started writing down Bianca's name when my pen ran out of ink. "Ugh. I need another pen. Let me grab one from my purse."

Just then I remembered those darn purses in the back seat of my car. I could just hear Dave saying, "Don't ever leave valuables in plain sight in the car overnight. It's an invitation to get your car window broken by a thief." I jumped up and grabbed my keys. "I forgot something in the car, I'll be right back."

Heaving the big trash bag full of purses over my shoulder, I locked the car and lugged the bag up the front steps, dropping it on the living room floor with a loud clunk.

"What on earth do you have in there, a bowling ball?" Kelly laughed.

"These are the purses that Janice donated for the auction. They've been in my car since yesterday morning, just before Sam and I discovered Gino's body. Let's take a break and see if there are any treasures in the bag we might want to bid on."

"Sounds good to me." Kelly rubbed her palms together. "I do love a good bargain."

I untied the knot in the top of the bag and dumped the whole lot in the middle of the living room floor. Again, we heard the loud clunk as about eight purses fell out–followed by a gun.

Kelly screamed, and we both stared at it like it was an alien spaceship.

"Don't touch it. I'm calling Hunt," I said, already pressing the call.

I was pretty sure it was probably the murder weapon and Hunt agreed. Whoever shot Gino probably thought it was a bag of trash to be taken to the dumpster and no one would ever be the wiser. He took the gun and the bag to be tested for fingerprints and left us with a floor full of purses. I walked him out to his car.

"I'm sorry for the way I acted at lunch today." I looked into his blue gray eyes. "If you say you didn't follow me, I believe you."

"Glory, I was as shocked as you were when the reality occurred to me today that your Dave was *the* Dave Harper. It's a time in my life I was forced to put behind me."

"And it's a time in my life I have chosen to put behind me. I loved Dave, but I realize I never really knew him. I just gave up fighting the system and moved on."

"Can you give us a chance knowing that I know all I know?"

"Somehow, it's comforting to know that you already know everything. I don't have to avoid it and I don't have to explain it."

"That's a lot of 'knows.'" He chuckled and lifted my chin to look into my eyes. "So, is that a yes?" He smiled that darned dimpled smile.

"Oh, it's definitely a yes." I wrapped my arms around his neck and stood on my tiptoes. He reached around my waist and pulled me close and our lips met. I laid my head against his chest, and I could feel his heart beating as fast as mine.

I looked up and asked, "Do you have a time of death yet?"

He smiled and said, "Yeah, Sherlock. 10:30."

And I smiled back.

When I walked back into the house, Kelly had already picked up all the purses, setting aside a few favorites for me to see, and put them in a new trash bag. The door opened and Macy and Tony walked in.

"Hey, you two. How was supper?" I asked, hoping to lift their dragging spirits.

"It was good. We went down to Lake House Café and shared a burger and basket of fries. Neither of us was really hungry."

Tony walked to the sofa and sat as Macy followed. "Have you heard any news today? Am I still a suspect?"

Kelly and I sat to join them. "I haven't been able to get much out of either Jake or Hunt today, but I did find out that time of death has been determined as approximately 10:30 yesterday morning."

"Well," Tony said, "that's about the time I was stopped for coffee just outside Baileyville, but how does that help us if I can't produce a receipt?"

"At least we know where you were at the time of the murder and it was nowhere close to the scene. Maybe we can figure out a way to prove it. Do you think the coffee shop had security cameras?"

"I seriously doubt it." Tony said shaking his head. "It was just a little hole in the wall. I'd be shocked if they did."

I picked up my notebook and added a reminder to take a drive to Baileyville tomorrow if I could get away. Maybe Pastor Dan would be okay with me coming in little late tomorrow morning, if I got there by lunch. I was sure he wouldn't mind as long as I had everything ready for tomorrow night's service and activities.

We filled Macy and Tony in on how we found the gun. "Surely that will help clear your name. Do you even own a gun?"

"No, I don't. I saw enough killing growing up around the family. My dad steered me clear of all that. Now, granted, I can do some damage with a knife, but I hate guns."

I cringed at the thought and was thankful at that moment that Gino wasn't stabbed.

"Have you heard back from your dad?" I asked Tony.

"Yes, he called this afternoon. He spoke with Aunt Celia and she told him some surprising news. It seems that Gino and Bianca have been separated for a couple of months, because Gino has been messing around with my Aunt Rosalind. That's my Uncle Rocco's wife."

"Weren't Gino and Rocco friends?"

"Yes, Gino was like family. When my grandfather found out, he disavowed Gino from the family. That's when Gino came down here. I figure to give Rocco and Papa time to cool off."

I took a minute to let that sink in. "So, you're telling me that the woman I met today has actually been separated from Gino for months, because he was messing around on her with their best friend's wife?"

"Aunt Celia also said that rumor has it that Gino had already contacted a lawyer and was about to file for divorce."

"Well, well, well. And I just thought the soon-to-be-ex-Mrs. Moretti didn't have a strong enough motive. If she was about to lose her sugar daddy in a divorce settlement, she may have figured, why take the chance on only getting half in a divorce when she could get it all with him dead."

"And that only works if he's dead before the divorce." Kelly added as she got up and took her tea glass to the kitchen. I followed her cue, picked up my glass and trailed behind her.

"Are you going to tell Macy about Hunt's connection to Dave?" she whispered.

"I will. Just not tonight. We all have enough to worry about without opening that can of worms with her."

"I take it you and Hunt are okay?"

"Yes, we're more than okay." I could feel my face turning pink.

"I'm glad! I'll see you tomorrow night at church?"

"You know I'll be there! I'm working tomorrow at the church, but I think I'll call Pastor Dan and ask him if he minds if I take the morning off. I'm thinking of taking a drive to Baileyville for a cup of coffee."

Kelly said goodnight to Macy and Tony and headed home.

"I think I'm going to bed, kids. It's been a crazy day," I said as I turned off the music and picked up my phone.

I turned to Tony. "Don't you worry about this, Tony. It's all gonna work out. Jake and Hunt are good at their jobs, and they won't stop until the truth comes out. I promise we are going to do all we can to make sure that's sooner rather than later."

Tony smiled. For the first time since this whole thing started, he actually looked like he believed me. I just hoped I could make good on that promise.

THIRTEEN

M acy had already left for the bakery when my alarm went off. Izzy must have been as tired as I was, because she never made a peep. I fluffed up my pillows, propped myself up in the bed and reached for the Bible on my bedside table. Izzy snuggled up next to my leg and snored. With so much on my mind, I needed some focus to start this crazy day ahead of me.

"Trust in the Lord with all your heart, and do not lean on your own understanding. In all your ways acknowledge him, and he will direct your paths." Proverbs 3:5-6

Wow. I needed that reminder. After reading several more verses, I said a quick prayer for guidance for Jake and Hunt as well as myself as we tried to help clear Tony's name and find the real killer roaming our small town.

After a quick shower, I pulled on a cute maxi length dress with a wide belt and some black sandals. I made sure Izzy had everything she needed and headed to the bakery for my morning coffee. Pastor Dan had been fine with me taking the morning off, so I planned to drive to Baileyville to see if there was any way to verify Tony's alibi.

When I walked into the bakery, I saw that the regular crew was already settled in at their table. This morning's game of choice was some type of cards.

"Mornin' Glory!" Momma chirped as she bagged up a couple of sinfully sweet looking apple turnovers for the customer at the counter.

I poured myself my usual iced coffee and went over to say hello to the men. "Good morning, fellas. How are things with y'all this lovely day?"

"Good morning, Glory!" they all said in unison.

"What's the matter, don't you guys trust each other?" I said, noticing. They all four had carefully placed their cards face down on the table and given each other the side-eye.

"Not as far as I can throw these old goats!" Leo declared.

Jimmy Don motioned for me to come a little closer. "Glory, I heard through the grapevine that you were doing your own investigation of the murder." He glanced knowingly across the room at Momma. I frowned at her, and she shrugged and gave me a sheepish grin.

"My cousin Gene owns a boat rental place over in the next county. We were talking last night about the murder and all the goings on around here lately. He said what with all the Yankees coming down from up north lately, we shouldn't expect any less."

"Yankees? Other than Gino, who would he have seen from up north?"

"Gene said something real curious. He said that some guy with New York tags rented a boat, but the crazy thing was that he wanted to leave his car stored at Gene's place. When Gene told him that he needed to have a local address on file for the rental, he said he was staying at Jamison Cabins #2 and he would be using the boat for most of his gettin' around."

"Jamison Cabins?" I looked at the other men. "Are y'all familiar with them?"

"That's old Fred Jamison's shacks. He's got two or three little one room places he rents out to campers and fishermen. I think most of them are somewhere in the woods off County Road 42. Somewhere around the Robinson Cut-Off," Leo said.

"My nephew stayed in one of them last spring when he came over from Atlanta for a fishing trip." Billy chimed in. "If you turn left at Robinson Cut-Off and go about three miles, there's a dirt road that veers off where the old Free State Barn used to be. Turn there and go about another mile. All three cabins are around there somewhere. A couple are up more in the woods, but there's one right on the water."

"That would have to be the one he's in, don't you think? Since he left his car at Gene's place and is going in and out by water," I reasoned.

"Sounds about right." Jimmy Don agreed. "Now don't you be going out in the forest all by yourself. You need to be smart about this."

"Oh, don't worry. I'll be sure to be careful. Thank you for the inside scoop. Maybe this is just what we need to break the case," I said, as Jimmy Don puffed up like a proud old rooster.

The drive to Baileyville wasn't particularly interesting. This stretch of road was nothing but chicken houses and hay fields. I saw mile after mile of huge round bales awaiting pickup by farmers for their livestock and other uses. When I reached the Baileyville City Limits sign, I started looking for the little café Tony had described. All he could remember is that it was on the left side of the road and that the name of the café had a woman's name in it. After passing a place on the right called Joe's Burger Joint, followed by a gas station, I saw it. Up ahead on the left was Dot's Diner. That had to be it. I pulled the car into the half-full parking lot and got out. Dot's Diner was a tiny, greasy little place with a counter and five stools and maybe five booths in the whole room. Barely big enough to swing a dead cat in. And from the looks of the place, I wouldn't be surprised if that had actually happened. The waitress behind the counter was ringing up a couple of coffees to go for two customers on their way out so I waited my turn in line.

"What can I get you?" the waitress, Marlene, or so her tag read, asked me in a raspy voice. Her greasy hair was yanked tight in a ponytail. A once-white apron sporting a myriad of food stains was tied around her ample waist. I hated not to order something, but I couldn't stomach the thought of food prepared there if the kitchen didn't look any cleaner than the counter.

"I'll just take a cup of coffee—to go." I said, thinking the Styrofoam would be safer than drinking from a coffee cup.

"You got it." Her smile showed the absence of at least two teeth in front.

She returned with my coffee. "I'd like to ask you a question if you can spare a minute."

"Sure thing." She leaned on the counter and wiped her hands on her apron.

"Were you working here on Monday morning?"

"Yep. I'm here every morning. I own this place." She swept out her hand like she was surveying her kingdom. I was a little confused. If she was the owner and her name was Marlene, who was Dot? I decided to let it go.

"A friend of mine came in for coffee at about 10:30 Monday morning. He's in a bit of a pickle and someone thinks he did something he didn't do. We're just trying to find someone who can verify he was here, and not somewhere else. Do you happen to remember him? He's a little taller than me, brown curly hair, in his late thirties. He was driving a gray SUV. I know that's not much to go on, but I'm hoping you will remember him."

"Sorry. I don't remember anybody like that. But if I remember rightly, Monday was the day Sam didn't show up for work and I had to work the grill all day. Letha was working out front Monday, but she ain't here today. Sorry, I can't help your friend none."

My heart sank as I paid her for the coffee and thanked her for her time. I walked out into the 98% Alabama humidity realizing I had wasted a whole morning for a crappy cup of coffee. I looked across the street and noticed a bank. Not only a bank, but an ATM. And ATMs have security cameras. If I could convince them to let me see the footage from Monday, maybe, just maybe, it would show the patrons of Dot's Diner. I walked across the street and into the cool bank lobby.

"Good morning! Can I help you?" A perky young teller asked from behind her station.

"I hope so. Who might I talk to, to get permission to see your ATM security camera footage?"

A look of complete confusion came across her face. "Well, I'm not sure. I'll have to check with our manager. I'll be right back."

Shortly, she reappeared with a pudgy, balding gentleman trailing behind.

"Beth tells me you want to see security camera footage?"

I nodded. "Yes, sir. Would that be possible? I need to see footage from Monday morning around 10:30."

"May I ask why you need to see it?"

I proceeded to explain Tony's predicament. After a lot of cajoling, the manager gave in. He seemed sympathetic to our plight and asked me to follow him down a hall and through a door marked EMPLOYEES ONLY. He logged into a computer and pulled up data, selecting Monday's date from a list. He scanned through the video until he arrived at 10:15, then slowed down as we watched cars pass on the street. Some pulled into the bank lot and some you could see across the street at Dot's. I just hoped that Tony parked in plain view of the camera. After scanning through another thirty minutes with no sign of Tony, we were about to give up, when at 10:43, Tony's gray Subaru Outback pulled in and parked at Dot's. I watched as Tony went into the diner and came back out at almost 11:00 with a coffee cup in hand. He got into the car and exited the lot. The bank manager paused the video at several points and allowed me to take screenshots with my phone of Tony with the time stamp clearly visible.

I thanked him profusely and left the bank. I was ecstatic as I got back in my car and headed back to town. I drove through Moody's and grabbed a grilled chicken wrap and a Diet Coke to eat at my desk. When I pulled into the church parking lot, I sent both Jake and Hunt a text with the pictures attached. I knew they wouldn't be happy with me and I was sure to get a lecture, but I was pretty proud of myself. I also sent Macy the pictures and told her to let Tony know he could finally breathe easy.

FOURTEEN

After inhaling my lunch, I made a quick call to Brigette at Busy Bee Florist to confirm my order for Sunday's flower arrangement for the sanctuary, checked off a few more boxes and finished up my usual responsibilities for tonight's mid-week service and activities. I was typing up the sermon outline for the Sunday bulletin when my phone buzzed a text from Hunt.

"Good job, Sherlock. Now let it go. Too dangerous."

"Thanks. Church supper? Chicken tenders tonight. Sabrina's honey mustard is the best."

Our church cook made the best honey mustard in three states. We had repeatedly encouraged her to market it as Sabrina's Liquid Gold, but she wouldn't give in.

"Tied up here till late. Anyway, could you bring me and Jake a couple of to-go plates? We'd be forever grateful."

"I think I can do that for such hard-working peace officers. Kelly's teaching children's choir class, but I'll be there around 6:00. Will that work?"

"Perfect. Looking forward to it—and the chicken too." Followed by a kissy lip emoji.

My heart smiled.

I logged out of my computer, closed up the office for the day and made my way down the hall to the kitchen at about 5:00. I saw Momma just getting in the meal line, so I slid in with her.

"How was your day at the bakery?" I touched Momma on the elbow, and she jumped out of her skin.

"Oh, Glory! You sneaked up on me! It was a good day at the bakery! Steady stream of business most of the day."

"Where's Macy? Is she coming to supper here at the church?"

"I left her still baking at about 3:30. I think she said that she and Tony would be here to eat. I'm sure they'll be along in a few minutes."

"I have been asked to deliver take out plates to Jake and Hunt at the station, so I'm getting mine to go."

She leaned close and asked, "Speaking of our police force, do we have any news on the investigation?"

I lowered my voice to a whisper, "I took the morning off and drove to Baileyville. I was able to verify Tony's alibi, so I think he's finally in the clear. I just wish we had enough on any of the other suspects to make an arrest."

"Did you say *we*? I figured once Tony was cleared, you would bow out of this one." Momma grinned. "But I can see by the look on your face, that's not the case is it? You're in too deep and just can't let it go."

I shrugged. "I do have a couple more leads to follow up on. I'll be careful and pass on anything I find out to Hunt and Jake."

"Let me know if you need a sidekick."

"You know I will!" I said, as Macy and Tony walked up to the serving line.

They both looked much better than the last time I'd seen them. I was thankful Tony's name was out of the investigation.

I just hoped that any family ties that were found, didn't throw suspicion back on him.

I had the ladies load up three take-out containers with chicken, fries and some of those mouth-watering cheesy ranch biscuits Sabrina makes. They added a nice big helping of liquid gold and a jug of sweet tea for us to share. In addition to the best honey mustard around, Sabrina also had the best sweet tea. I didn't know how she did it, but it was always perfect. Somewhere between wannabe sweet and pour-it-over-your-pancakes-when-you're-out-of-syrup sweet. I left the parking lot slowly, careful not to take the turns too sharply. I didn't want any chicken casualties on the way to the station.

I had texted Hunt that I was on my way, so he was watching for me and came out to help me carry all the goodies inside.

Most everyone had gone home for the night, including the not-so-friendly desk clerk that had greeted me on occasion. In fact, Jake had cleaned off her desk and turned it into an eating space for the three of us.

"I have a feeling this lady is not gonna like the smell of fried chicken at her desk tomorrow morning. She already hates me." I looked around for a better place to set up supper.

"Who? Connie? She's a pushover! She likes to put on a tough front, but she's a sweetheart." Jake laughed.

"Well, just the same, don't mention my name when she questions the greasy spots on her desk calendar in the morning." I figured I'd just go ahead and address the elephant in the room before it got too awkward. "How's the investigation coming?"

They glanced at each other, and Jake let out a roaring "Whoop!" that scared the life out of me.

"What in the world was that all about?" I asked.

Hunt grimaced as he reached into his back pocket and pulled out his wallet. He took out a one-dollar bill and reluctantly handed it to Jake. Jake set down his glass of iced tea and gleefully snatched the dollar out of Hunt's hand. He grasped each end of the bill with his hands, popping it tight in the air a couple of times before he neatly folded it up and stuck it in his shirt pocket. "Jake bet me a dollar that you wouldn't last five minutes after you got here before you'd bring up the murder," Hunt explained, and I glared at Jake.

"I thought surely you'd at least ask us how our day had been before you stuck your nose right in," Hunt said indignantly.

"Glad I could provide your evening entertainment, guys." I could feel my face getting redder, but I might as well see if I could wheedle any information out of them since I'd already opened that can of worms. "So, now that Tony's in the clear, who else are you looking at?"

"Glory, you know we're not going to discuss police business with you." Hunt looked pointedly at me with a stern gaze. "We do appreciate you telling us about the bank camera footage, but that's as far as you go. Like I told you earlier. It's too dangerous."

I confess that one of my faults is a very large stubborn streak, and it picked that moment to rear its ugly head. If he wasn't going to share information with me, then he wouldn't get anything from me either.

"If that's the way it's gotta be, then that's the way it's gotta be." I shrugged nonchalantly. Jake immediately gave me the side eye, letting me know he wasn't falling for my act.

"Macy's business is really doing great. She's already building up a loyal group of customers," I commented, deciding that changing the subject might be a better tactic.

They both looked up at me, each with a chicken finger in their hand frozen in a mid-dip of liquid gold. A look of disbelief crossed their faces that I would move on in the conversation without putting up a fight.

"Uh... That's great!" Jake said. "I knew she would do a great job. I hear people talking all over town about how much they love it."

I took a sip of my sweet iced tea. "There's the funniest group of old retirees that have been coming in every morning. They have their coffee and share a big basket of Macy's muffins and play some kind of game. One day it's dominoes and the next it's rummy. One of them is on the city council." I glanced over at the guys to see if that bit of information registered with them. Nope. Not a blink.

"That's nice," Hunt said as he popped a French fry in his mouth.

"These old guys are pretty sharp and know just about everything that goes on in town. It's like a male version of Bonnie's Cut and Curl. In fact, Bonnie June's husband is one of them."

"I wouldn't put much stock in what a bunch of old men have to say. They're as bad as women to stretch the truth." Jake stopped and jerked his head up. "I mean ...sometimes they...well, they like to..."

I loved to watch my brother squirm. "I guess you're right. Maybe I should just take it all with a grain of salt."

Both guys nodded sheepishly. We ate in silence for the next few minutes, thoroughly enjoying Sabrina's home cooking.

"Well, I think I'd better head home. Got a busy day tomorrow," I said as I gathered the trash, making sure we didn't leave any trace of chicken on Connie's desk or in her trash can. Jake thanked me for bringing the supper, and I waved goodbye as I walked toward the door.

"Will you be working at the bakery tomorrow?" Hunt asked, as he joined me, walking out.

"I'll be there, bright and early. Will you come by in the morning for coffee?"

"I wouldn't miss it. I can't start my day without your smile." He leaned down and gave me a quick, soft kiss. He opened my car door and waited while I settled in and buckled up.

"Be safe." He smiled and his eyes sparkled in the streetlight. That dimple. Ugh. How was I ever gonna stay mad at that?

"You too." I smiled. "See you in the morning."

FIFTEEN

It was a quick drive home. Both Macy's and Tony's cars were in the driveway. I opened the door to find them snuggled on the sofa, engrossed in an episode of a cooking show with a bowl of popcorn between them. Izzy was curled up next to Macy sound asleep.

"Hi, Mom!" Macy said with a relaxed smile.

I was so glad to see both of them looking more at ease than they had in the last few days. I hoped that what I was about to tell them didn't send Tony over the edge again. I waited until the episode finished, then decided to share my latest information with them.

Macy got up to refill their tea glasses.

"I just had supper at the station with Uncle Jake and Chief Walker. They were as relieved as we were to see the bank camera footage," I said, taking a seat in the chair opposite the sofa.

"Thank you again, Mrs. Harper, for going out of your way to help clear me," Tony said.

"Please, call me Glory. And you are so welcome." I shifted in my chair and tucked my foot up under me. "I have some more news that I gathered from your group of regulars this morning at the bakery."

"Good news or bad news?" Macy lifted an eyebrow.

"I think that may be up to Tony to decide." I looked over at him to see a frown come across his face.

I relayed the story that Jimmy Don had told me about his cousin Gene's boat rental establishment in the neighboring county and how he rented a boat to a guy with a New York car tag.

Tony's face paled. "Did he give you a name?"

"He didn't say. Just that the guy parked his car out of sight and intended to use the boat for most of his coming and going to the place he was renting."

"When did he rent the boat? How long has he been in town?" Macy asked.

"He didn't know. We can ask Jimmy Don in the morning if his cousin told him any other details we can use."

Tony's brow furrowed. "This isn't good. I need to call my dad and see if the family has sent someone down here. If my grandfather was mad enough at Gino, he could've sent someone down to take care of the problem."

"But this could be good, right?" Macy looked expectantly at Tony. "I mean, if someone was sent down here, maybe they're the one who killed Gino, and all this will be over soon."

Tony shook his head. "I have spent my whole life trying to disassociate myself from that side of my family. I really don't want that stigma hanging over me or my business. I just want to live my life like any other normal person."

"We'll cross that bridge when we come to it." I assured him in an effort to give him a little peace of mind. "Meanwhile, why don't you get some sleep and we'll try to get more information tomorrow."

"I'll see you in the morning. Izzy and I are gonna turn in." I let Izzy out into the backyard one last time for the evening then we both called it a night.

As soon as I climbed into bed, I knew I wasn't going to be able to sleep. Tony's statement about normal people's lives and getting away from his past kept haunting me. I wanted to tell him that most families aren't as normal as they seem. We all have secrets and parts of lives we wish we could leave behind. I thought of my own convoluted connection to the mob through Dave's murder. If he and Macy decided to take the next step toward marriage, I knew we'd have to fill him in on all our dirty laundry. But, right now, I wanted him to find some kind of normalcy with us that could calm his anxious mind and give him someone to lean on.

Deciding to read for a while, I opened the Bible app on my phone.

"Gently encourage the stragglers and reach out for the exhausted, pulling them to their feet. Be patient with each person, attentive to individual needs. And be careful that when you get on each other's nerves you don't snap at each other. Look for the best in each other, and always do your best to bring it out." 1 Thessalonians 5:13-15. *(The Message)*

I thought about how many areas of my life that verse pointed to these days. I wanted to be an encouragement to Tony and to Macy and I also needed to be careful to be patient and not snap at Jake and Hunt in frustration when they refused to include me in the progress of the investigation.

I must have been more exhausted than I realized, because the next thing I knew, I woke to the sound of Macy easing my bedroom door open to let Izzy out for the morning. My bedside light was still on and my phone still in my hand. I groggily thanked her and threw off the blanket. After a quick shower, I was ready for a day of following up leads. Of course, all that would have to wait until the bakery closed at 3:00. I glanced at the collection of multi-colored sticky notes arranged on my bathroom mirror. I was perpetually absent-minded. Another in a long list of character traits I wasn't that proud of. This morning, I only had two notes, which was hopefully, a good sign. "Question Jimmy Don" and "Find Jamison Cabins."

I grabbed my notebook, purse and keys and joined Macy who was already sitting in the car talking on her phone. She ended the call as I got in and buckled up.

"That was Tony. He said he left a message for his dad last night but hasn't heard back yet. I take it that it must be a pretty big deal for him to get in touch with Tony's grandfather. It doesn't sound like they are on speaking terms, so he may have to go through his Aunt Celia again to get any information. He said they usually respond on their own timetable, so we'll just have to wait until we hear."

"Okay. Meanwhile, I plan to go ahead and talk to Jimmy Don this morning. Hopefully, he might know more than he told me yesterday. I may take another drive out to the motel and see if Bianca knows anything about this mystery person from up north. There's no way it's a coincidence. They all have to be connected to Gino in some way. North Alabama didn't suddenly become a mecca for New York vacationers."

All the stores along Main Street were still dark. The only lights were the scattered decorative streetlamps boasting banners about the Labor Day Boat Parade on the lake next weekend. Not wanting to take up valuable customer parking on the front, I parked in the small parking lot behind the bakery and we entered through the kitchen entrance. Macy went up front and turned off the alarm system. I got a couple of coffeemakers started while she mixed up the recipe for the Special of the Day, chocolate chip scones.

"Mom, who do you really think killed Gino?" Macy asked.

"I'm sure there could be other suspects that I'm not aware of, but the ones on my list are Chris Lester or one of the other landowners, like maybe Jeff Newsome, the soon-to-be-ex wife, Bianca and now, maybe this unknown "family member" from New York."

"Let's look at each one and see what feels like the best place to start."

Just then, I heard a knock on the door out front. I swung the door from the kitchen open enough to see Kelly standing on the sidewalk peering through the glass doors. I wiped my hands on the towel tucked in my apron and unlocked the door.

"What on earth are you doing out this early in the morning? It's barely 5:30." I ushered her in and locked the door behind her.

"I just couldn't sleep, and I knew you two would be here getting ready to open, so I decided to come by. I thought maybe we could have an impromptu meeting of the Crime Club while we work." Kelly's eyes sparkled expectantly.

"You must be psychic. Macy and I were just about to go over our suspect list and see what the next step should be. I think the coffee should be ready by now. Pour yourself a cup and come back into the kitchen and we'll get started."

When Kelly and I were young, we both loved to read mysteries. We would read the same book and compete to see who could solve the mystery first. We called it our Crime Club. I never dreamed that so many years later, we would be trying to solve real mysteries. It's much more sobering to know that someone's actual life and future could be at stake. It's not all fun and games anymore.

Kelly joined us in the kitchen and pulled up a stool to the stainless prep table where Macy and I were working. I motioned a flour-coated hand toward my suspect notebook poking its head out of my bag.

"Grab my notebook so you can jot down anything we need to remember."

She pulled out a pen and the notebook, turning to a fresh page and sat ready to write.

SIXTEEN

"Okay, first let's look at Chris Lester. We know it's no secret around town how he feels about the condo project. He's been very vocal at the City Council meeting as well as to me when we met Tuesday. His wife has even said on occasion things that could be taken as threats toward Terrance. I also heard her tell Cindy Newsome that they may not have to worry about the problem much longer."

"That could mean any number of things," Kelly said, taking a sip of coffee. "The first thing that comes to mind is that she had knowledge that her husband had a plan to stop the project."

"That could mean he was going to blow the top off Gino's shady past and possibly cause Terrance to lose his biggest financial backer," I said.

"Or it could mean he was going to take Gino out of the equation for good," Macy added.

I kneaded the scone dough onto the floured table and started cutting it into triangles.

"According to Lester, he was scheduled to meet Gino Monday morning at 10:00 at the motel, but Gino wasn't there. I see several possible scenarios here," I continued, as Kelly scribbled in the notebook. "Maybe Lester lied, and Gino was at the motel. Lester killed Gino at the motel and moved his body to the construction site in Gino's car. He got nervous when I asked him if he knew how to drive a stick shift. That's the point in our conversation when he made sure I saw the gun in his desk drawer. So, we know that he can handle a gun and he owns one. He could have gotten his wife to come pick him up out at the site and take him back to the motel to pick up his own car."

"Wouldn't Bianca have been aware of anything that happened in that motel room? Why would she protect Chris Lester by covering for him?" asked Kelly.

"Maybe Gino instructed Bianca to take a walk so they could have a private visit or something," Macy added.

I thought for a few minutes as I neatly placed the scones onto the sheet pans, slid the pans into the oven and wiped off my hands.

"I haven't heard Jake or Hunt mention if they have determined the actual murder scene yet, but I know it wasn't at the location the body was found. There was no blood or evidence of a struggle anywhere near, except of course on Gino himself." I took out my phone and flipped through the pictures that I took at the construction site the day we found the body.

"Wow! I totally forgot about this!" I said, showing my phone to both Macy and Kelly. "I noticed what looked like drag marks from the office trailer to the body, so I'm willing to bet that the murder happened in or near the trailer."

"So how or why did they end up at the construction site instead of the motel?" Macy asked, placing two pans of cranberry nut muffins she'd just mixed up into the other oven and setting the timer.

"One possibility might be that since Gino didn't want Bianca around for the meeting, when Lester arrived, they moved the meeting to the offices." Kelly tapped the pencil on her chin thoughtfully. "Maybe Lester followed Gino to the offices to have their meeting and that's how Gino's car ended up at the work site."

"Do you think that Chris Lester was planning to kill Gino all along? Was that the purpose of the meeting to begin with?" Macy asked.

Kelly frowned. "I know Chris Lester can be a hardheaded businessman and maybe sketchy to deal with, but I don't see him as a cold-blooded killer. I mean, they're such upstanding members of the community. Why would he risk that over some land value? If it's that important to them, they could just put their house on the market and build on another section of the lake. They have plenty of money to do that."

"I see your point. But what if it wasn't pre-meditated? Maybe Chris was just planning to use all the dirt he had uncovered on Gino to get him to back out of the deal so that Terrance would lose everything. It's his way of killing two birds with one stone. He gets the project stopped for his precious land values, and he destroys Terrance financially. It's no secret that he and Terrance don't get along."

Kelly nodded, "That sounds a lot more plausible. He was, in essence, blackmailing Gino in order to get him to back out of the project."

"Exactly," I agreed. "But he didn't realize who he was dealing with. I'm sure the 'family' doesn't take well to threats of blackmail. He underestimated Gino and thought he would turn tail and run, but maybe Gino decided to call Lester's bluff."

Macy pulled up a stool to the prep table. "What if Gino pulled a gun on Lester, they struggled and somehow Lester got the gun away from Gino and shot him in self-defense? Maybe it was just a blackmailing scheme that escalated and went off the rails."

We all three sat back and smiled, feeling pretty proud of our sleuthing skills at the moment.

"I need some coffee, and then we can talk about suspect number two, Mrs. Moretti." I said exiting through the swinging door into the bakery.

"Bring me a cup, Mom!" shouted Macy, as I poured myself an iced coffee.

I poured her a cup of her favorite with a splash of vanilla creamer and carried them back into the kitchen.

I glanced at the clock. We had about another half hour before we needed to get moving for the day and open for business. Kelly flipped to the next page in the notebook and wrote Bianca's name at the top.

"What do we know about Bianca Moretti?" she asked.

"According to Josie Johnson at the motel, she arrived sometime Saturday night, even though she has lied to the police and to me about when she got into town. Josie said she had not physically seen who was in the room with Gino, but she assumed it was a woman from the scent of perfume. Bianca had been careful to stay out of sight, yet she hadn't bothered to hide her Lexus SUV. Josie and I thought that odd, but it may just be that she's not that smart. She did strike me as a little ditzy and over dramatic. She has to know that Jake or Hunt will find out the truth from Josie, if they haven't already."

"She wants everyone to think that she just arrived after being contacted by the police to come down and identify Gino's body, but obviously she was here for a different reason. Why do you think she was here?" Kelly asked

"My impression of her was that she is a spoiled, rich wife who wanted me to believe she was mourning the loss of the love of her life, but in truth, she sounded like she was going to miss his money a lot more than she was going to miss him. I would love to know if they had a pre-nup."

Kelly pulled out her laptop and set it up on the prep table. "I think pre-nup agreements are a matter of public record. I don't know why I didn't think of that before," She said, continuing to search.

"Tony's dad talked to his Aunt Celia and told him that Gino's been messing around on Bianca. Maybe she came down to try to win him back." Macy blew across the top of her coffee then took a sip.

"If that was her intention, why all the secrecy? Why not just be honest about when you got to town?" Kelly wondered.

"Maybe she's just embarrassed that she couldn't keep her husband. That probably carries a major stigma in the bubble she lives in." I got up from the stool and peeked into the ovens to check the muffins and the scones. "And what's worse is that she was losing him to Gino's best friend's wife. That had to be tough. I don't know if she and Bianca were friends, but you know everyone in the 'family' had to know about it."

"Yes, because Aunt Celia said that Gino had recently contacted a lawyer to start the process to file for divorce." Macy said.

"That may have been the last straw. Maybe that's what made her desperate enough to drive all the way down here from New York alone to try to talk some sense into him." Kelly continued to add to the notes on the Bianca page of the notebook.

"It also may have made her desperate enough to kill him. If she realized she couldn't talk any sense into him, she may have figured it was better for her if he died before the divorce. That way she would get it all instead of just half."

"Correction—not half. Try zero." Kelly looked up from her computer. "I just found a pre-nup agreement filed in New York courts in 2010 stating that in the event of divorce between Gino Moretti and Bianca Canale Moretti within fifteen years from the date of marriage, all assets are retained by Mr. Moretti."

I canoodled that for a hot minute. "So that means she would have had to put up with his tomcatting for at least five more years to get even half of his money."

"Do you think she's smart enough to pull all this off? How did she get him to the construction site? Would she be strong enough to drag him all the way from the trailer to the place where you found Gino?" Macy made a good point.

"I don't know. I hadn't thought about that. Gino was a big guy and that's got to be at least a hundred yards from the trailer to ground zero, as Sam called it," I said, looking back at the photos on my phone.

"Well, she definitely had motive and we know she can handle a gun, as evidenced by the way she waved it in your face. I'm just not so sure about opportunity." Kelly took a quick sip of her coffee. "If we thought he was killed in the motel, then yes, but out at the site, I'm not convinced."

"I agree, but she's still high on my list," I said, and Macy and Kelly agreed.

"Okay, we've got a few more minutes before I need to turn the sign and unlock the front door. Who else is on the list?" Macy asked.

"We have an unknown 'Yankee from up north' that Jimmy Don's cousin, Gene, rented a boat to. I have no idea if it's connected to the investigation, and I thought I might see if I can get any more information out of Jimmy Don this morning when the regulars come in. It could be totally unrelated, but my gut tells me it's too much of a coincidence."

They both nodded and we agreed to talk more tonight over supper at my place. Since I had moved back from Texas, it had become a weekly thing to share supper with Jake and Kelly. We would alternate weeks at each other's homes. Lately, Hunt had been added to the mix as had Tony and Macy on occasion, unless the youngsters had better things to do than to eat with the old folks. Tonight, I had planned to grill out, but I was sure Jake and Hunt would be tied up with the investigation. Since they considered themselves the grillmasters of our little group, I decided I should come up with an alternate menu.

"Mom, why don't you let me and Tony cook tonight? As a sort of thank you for helping clear his name in all this mess," Macy said, as she flipped the sign to OPEN and unlocked the door.

"That sounds wonderful!" I heard the oven ding and I rushed into the kitchen to pull out the morning's delicious offerings.

SEVENTEEN

As I arranged the warm Cranberry Walnut Muffins and Chocolate Chip Scones on the vintage trays for the display counter, I heard the first customers of the morning come through the door. I would recognize that deep voice anywhere.

"Good morning ladies," Hunt said. That killer smile with the dimple greeted me as I came through the swinging door with the trays of goodies. I was still caught off guard by the warm feeling I got all over when he walked into the room. I couldn't help but smile right back. I sure hoped I didn't look as googly eyed as I felt every time I saw him.

"Good morning, Hunt," I managed to mumble.

"Good morning to just Hunt? Am I invisible?" Jake feigned a heartbroken look.

"Sorry, brother! Good morning to you too!" I let out a nervous laugh. I hadn't even seen him standing next to Hunt. I must really have it bad.

"What are you doing here this early?" Jake looked questioningly at Kelly. "I really hope this is not what it looks like."

"And what would that be?" I asked defensively.

"This looks suspiciously like a Crime Club meeting." He looked at Kelly. "I knew you got up early, but I thought you were headed to the library to get some work done before it opened."

"I couldn't sleep, so I thought I would come down and help the girls get ready for the day," she said sheepishly.

"Sure, you did." He cocked an eyebrow and looked at all three of us. "I'm warning you girls, this is a dangerous one, and I...we", he said swishing his pointer finger back and forth between himself and Hunt, "will not allow you to get any more messed up in this than you already are."

"Is there anything you can tell us about how it's going?" I asked batting my eyes at Hunt. "I mean, I totally understand you can't share a lot, but I was the one that discovered poor Gino. Can you at least tell us if you've confirmed the place he was killed?"

Hunt rolled his eyes, "Okay, since you were there, and you were the one who pointed out the drag marks, I guess I can tell you that we did find evidence of a struggle in the back room of the office trailer and what was confirmed to be blood on the carpet. Someone had tried to clean it, but our team found enough to test."

"I knew it! And the blood was Gino's, right?" I squealed.

"Yes, Sherlock. You were right." He smiled.

"What about ballistics on the gun I found?" I asked, hoping he'd throw me one more bone.

"Results aren't back yet on that. We gotta get going." They took their coffees and turned for the door, effectively shutting down my inquisition.

"Try to stay out of trouble...especially you, Sherlock," Hunt said with a stern look.

"Yes, sir," I said with a mock salute and a smile.

On their way out the door, Jake and Hunt met Jimmy Don and the rest of the regulars coming in, and they held the door for the four retirees. "Good morning, gentlemen," Jake said. They nodded in greeting, one by one as they brushed past.

Hunt glanced over at me and repeated his stern gaze as if to give me one last reminder to be a good girl and mind my own business.

"Good morning!" I greeted. "Everyone getting their usual?"

"Morning. Coffee for me." Jimmy Don shuffled to his favorite chair.

"Same for me."

"Me, too."

"Hot and black." The other three responded in tandem.

I poured all their drinks, and, hoping I could butter them up for some more information about Gene's cousin this morning, I included a couple of the chocolate chip scones I had made that morning in their usual muffin basket. I arranged it all precariously on a tray and delivered it to the table. I was still honing my waitressing skills. "What's the game of the day, fellas?"

"Chicken foot," Leo said as he dumped the box of dominoes onto the table and flipped them all upside down.

"Saw your brother and his boss on our way in. Have they figured out who killed that Yankee, yet?" Jimmy Don asked.

I shrugged. "They're pretty tight-lipped since it's an ongoing investigation. I try to get them to talk, but it's like pulling hen's teeth."

"I finally talked to my cousin Gene again about the guy that rented his boat."

"Did you find out a name?"

"Well, all he could remember was Vinnie something."

My heart sank. "Didn't he keep a copy of a driver's license or something? Maybe he has a rental form?"

"Well, Cousin Gene ain't never been one for details. As long as you got cash money, he'll rent you a boat."

Leo started singing, under his breath, some song about his honey havin' the money and him havin' the time.

The other three started tapping the table and chimed in about going honky-tonkin' and havin' a time."

Trying to steer them back to the subject, "So, all he could remember was the name Vinnie?"

"You know in Alabama, you don't need a driver's license to rent a boat, and as long as you're fourteen, I think it is, you can drive one. I figure the Yankee must've looked at least fourteen years old, so Gene probably let the rest go. Like I said, he ain't never been much for details."

"I know he's your kin, Jimmy Don," Leo said, "but Gene's shady as they come."

Jimmy Don didn't seem to take offense. He just shrugged. "Can't choose your family."

"Okay, well, at least we have a name. Thanks for checking on it for me." I patted Jimmy Don on the shoulder. "Y'all let me know when you need a refill."

I just couldn't imagine renting out your boat to someone and not even getting the guy's last name, but I suppose he did have Vinnie's car. I guess he figured the guy had to bring the boat back to get the car, and if he didn't, well, good ol' Cousin Gene was just one car better off. And if it was as nice as Gino's and Bianca's, I'd say Gene would be better off if Vinnie kept the boat. What I couldn't figure out was, if Vinnie was in town to knock off Gino, then why was he still hanging around? He would have left after he did the job, unless he'd been told to do something else. Surely, they wouldn't be upset with Tony for any reason. Or maybe they were gonna tie up loose ends. Like Bianca? Maybe she knew too much. Or maybe there was just something about mob etiquette I didn't know.

I checked the stock on all the pastries and made sure the coffee pots were full, then headed to the kitchen to swap places with Macy so she could be out front with customers for a few hours. She handed me a couple of recipes to start working on. I appreciated her trusting me with some of the baking, knowing that it's not my strong suit. Momma and Macy were definitely the cooks in the family, but I was learning to hold my own.

Macy had finished peeling and slicing up a bowl full of fresh local peaches, and the kitchen smelled divine. Peaches were hands down, my favorite fruit, candle, tea, you name it. If it smelled like a peach, I loved it. Just as I started the big commercial KitchenAid mixer with the batter for three fresh peach pound cakes, I heard the bell on the front door jingle and Macy welcome them cheerily. I immediately recognized the New York accent and rushed over to sneak a peek through the small window in the swinging kitchen door. Sure enough, it was Bianca. Dressed to the nines in an expensive looking, navy blue strapless summer dress and bright red Jimmy Choo stilettos with lipstick to match.

"How do you people breathe in this oppressive heat down here?" she said fanning herself with one of the bakery menus. She pulled out a napkin from the dispenser on the counter and daintily dabbed at her ample chest cleavage.

I turned off the mixer and walked out into the bakery. "Oh! Hello, Bianca! I didn't know you were still in town." I walked over to where she was mulling over the bakery selections.

"What are you doing here? Do you work here?" She tried to keep the uneasy frown from forming on her botoxed forehead.

"My daughter owns this bakery. She's only been open a few weeks. Can I help you make a selection?"

"I think I'll take one of the chocolate chip scones and a large cup of the bold roast coffee, to go please."

I placed the scone in a bag along with a few napkins and poured her coffee.

"I've been down to see that cute police detective, and he has finally released my poor Gino's body so I can go home and put this whole horrible place behind me. I just thought I'd pick up a few things for the road."

"I didn't know they had finished their investigation. Have they made an arrest? I would think it would be all over town if they had found their man ...or woman," I said, with a slightly intentional air of accusation.

She cut her eyes over at me. "I hope you aren't implying that I had anything to do with Gino's death. I loved him." She glared intently. "I had everything I could ever need, more money than I could ever spend and a husband that worshipped the ground I walked on. What possible reason could I have for wanting him dead?"

I've heard it said that there are three main motives for murder. Love, money and revenge. It was clear Bianca had all three.

"Isn't it true that Gino was about to file for divorce? Hadn't he found a newer, younger model?"

"Where did you hear that? I don't know where you get your information, but it is absolutely not true."

"So, you're telling me he wasn't having an affair with his best friend's wife?"

Her body went rigid and she clenched her fists, visibly shaking. I could practically see the steam coming out of her ears. "That tramp followed my Instagram account," She hissed. "Every time she saw me post from some exotic vacation, she would conveniently remember something she had left at our home when she and Rocco were over visiting. She'd priss her little self over there, throwing herself at him. He was a man. What else do you expect?"

"So, you didn't blame him? He was the innocent victim in all of it? Is that why you came down here two days earlier than you told the police?"

Her penciled in eyebrows arched up. "How did you know that?"

"You didn't do a very good job of hiding it. I don't know if you've noticed, but we don't get a lot of visitors from New York. People around here notice car tags."

"At least I tried to give him the benefit of the doubt. That's why I came down here. To tell him that I forgive him."

"And what did he say?"

"He said he was sorry, and everything was going to be okay. We'd work it out. He told me to go back home and we'd discuss it when he finished his part of this job in a few weeks."

"I see. Can I ask you one more question?"

With an exasperated huff, she nodded. "What?"

"I heard there's another car in the area with New York plates. You wouldn't happen to know who that might be, do you?"

Her demeanor immediately changed. She was no longer the fiery, indignant socialite. Her face paled and her eyes went wide. She looked more like a terrified little girl. I knew immediately that she had no idea that Vinnie was here and what's more, she had no idea why. Regaining her composure, she straightened her shoulders. "I have no idea what you're talking about and I'm sure it has nothing to do with me."

I rang up her purchase, and she practically threw the money at me, then turned on her spikey little heel and walked out the door.

EIGHTEEN

M acy looked over at me wordlessly, still processing that exchange. Jimmy Don and the regulars were still in a heated game of chicken foot, and he motioned me over for a refill.

"Wooohweee! That's a hot one, there." He waved his hand toward the door. "You be careful, now, if you have any more dealings with her. She looks just a little too big for her britches."

I filled all their cups and nodded. "My Granny used to say, 'if you could buy her for what she's worth and sell her for what she thinks she's worth, you'd be a millionaire.'"

They all hooted and leaned back in their chairs.

Jimmy Don eyed me, "Well, I'm serious, Glory. I wouldn't trust her as far as I could throw her."

I headed straight back to the kitchen to finish up the peach pound cakes, but Macy had already filled the pans and was sliding them into the oven.

"Sorry, I got a little sidetracked," I apologized.

"It was definitely worth it to see her reaction! She was livid!" Macy said excitedly. "Do you think she did it, Mom?"

"I don't know. She has plenty of motive, but she seems so scatter-brained and air headed. I'm not sure she could pull it off. And to me, the bullet hole in the forehead screams mob hit, not irate, crazy jealous wife."

Macy went back out front while I started a couple of quiches for the lunch customers. I mulled over the suspect list of motives and opportunity while I filled a large pan with strips of bacon and placed it in the oven. While I cracked eggs, I dialed Hunt and put him on speaker.

"Hi, beautiful." His smooth voice gave me chills. "What's up?"

"Hey, you're never going to believe who was just in the bakery—Bianca Moretti," I said without giving him a chance to respond.

"Oh great. Please tell me you didn't play detective and interrogate her or anything."

"Not really interrogated. More like chatted," I winced. I could practically hear his eyes rolling. "She told me that you had released Gino's body and his car, and she was leaving town. Have you arrested someone? How can you release either of those until the case is closed?" I pulled out the cutting board and began dicing onion for the Quiche Lorraine.

"Whoa, slow down. First of all, no, we haven't made an arrest, but we don't need a body to do that. There's no mistaking what killed him, so there was no need for an autopsy. We collected all the evidence we could from the body itself, so we released it to be transported back."

"But what about the car?"

"The car has been gone over with a fine-tooth comb. There were only three sets of fingerprints in the car. Gino's, Terrance's and Sam's. Terrance and Sam both admit to being in the car. Sam rode with Gino to lunch at the Lake House Café one day and Terrance said that Gino took him for a spin in the sports car just to see what it could do. Janice confirmed both their stories. So, there is no reason to hold the car. And second of all—"

"But what about Bianca?" I interrupted. "Isn't she still a suspect? You know she's gonna leave town, don't you?"

He started again, "Glory, listen. Breathe. And second of all," he repeated emphatically, "I'm not going to tell you who's on our suspect list, but even if Bianca is still under suspicion, we don't have enough to hold her here."

"But you know she lied about when she came to town."

"Yes, we're aware of that and we questioned her about it. She gave us a satisfactory explanation for being in town. She was here to try and reconcile with her husband."

I stopped and took a deep breath, blew it out and continued slicing the gruyere and parmesan cheeses.

"Glory, I can't stress this enough. Please let us do our job and stop asking questions. People are already talking around town about how you are doing your own investigation—"

"Wait! What? Who's saying that?"

"I don't know. Beauty shops, coffee shops, library, church, restaurants, you name it. It's a small town. How do you expect gossip not to spread around about something like that? It sounds like you've become some kind of a sleuthing celebrity after that last mess you got yourself into."

I started to comment, but then closed my mouth.

"I worry about you. I can't help it. And if I have to spend my time worrying about you, that's less time I have to spend working on this case."

"I'm sorry, I'm distracting you." I couldn't help but smile to know that I was a just little bit distracting.

"Well, when this case is closed, you can distract me all you want," he whispered.

"Looking forward to it. Talk to you soon?"

"I'll call you later tonight. Maybe if we can get things wrapped up here at a decent hour, I could stop by, if that's okay with you?"

"I'd like that." I disconnected the call and put my phone away.

He was right. I needed to back off and let them do their job. And that's exactly what I was going to do. As soon as I followed up on one more little lead, I would leave it all to the professionals.

After combining all the ingredients, I gave it a good stir and poured the quiche mixtures into the pie crusts. I carefully slid them into the oven and set the timer. I washed my hands and went out front to help Macy get ready for the lunch crowd.

The rest of the afternoon passed quickly as we prepared tomorrow's specials and replenished the stock on our daily best sellers.

"Macy, have you talked to Tony today? Do you know if he has heard back from his dad about the mystery guy?"

"I texted him earlier, but he hasn't responded yet. I think he was doing the final walk through with the builder this morning at 10:00. I hope everything went well."

"Do you mind if I run next door and see if he's in? I'll be right back."

"Sure, Mom. I'm just getting ready to close out the register for the day."

I took off my apron and walked next door to Tavolo.

"Hi, Glory. I was just about to text Macy to see how her day went. I've been tied up with the builder most of the day and haven't had a chance to text her back."

"How did it go? Is everything still on schedule to open soon?"

"Yes, ma'am! Everything went great. I meet with the graphic designer Monday to sign off on the menu design, then they'll go to the printer. Everything is coming together. I'm so thankful."

"Were you able to talk to your dad about our mystery man?"

"I did text him this morning, but he still hasn't heard back from Aunt Celia. He said he tries to stay out of it, but if he had to guess, it's probably Vinnie Russo. Aside from Uncle Rocco, of course, he's Papa Angelo's right hand man."

"Jimmy Don's cousin Gene told us that the guy's name was Vinnie, but he didn't have a last name. That confirms it, then."

"You aren't planning on trying to talk to him, are you?"

"I thought I might take a ride out there and see if I can find that cabin. I just want to see if he's still there."

"Would you let me go with you? Hopefully, he'll be gone, and you won't even see him, but if you do, he might respond better if I'm with you. He may not even remember me, but at least I know how to handle the family situations. These people are very different than people from the south."

"I would like that. I'll let Macy know, and I'll meet you out back at the car as soon as you can get the place locked up."

"I'll be ready."

Macy wasn't thrilled that I wouldn't let her come along on our little road trip. I knew she had things to do at the bakery, but the main reason was that I needed her to stay in town. I told her I would check in with her when we found the cabin. I knew that if anything went sideways, we could call her, and she would have Jake and Hunt hot on our trail in a matter of minutes. I wasn't about to give them a heads up on our plans. They would have put a stop to it right quick and given me a lecture to boot. Better to ask forgiveness than permission, I always said.

NINETEEN

Tony met me in the alley behind the stores, and we climbed into his Subaru Outback, since we both knew it would take any back roads better than my Honda. I had tried to find Jamison Cabins online so I could enter them into the GPS on my phone, but no such luck. Old Fred Jamison must not put much stock in having an online presence. I'd just have to use the directions Jimmy Don gave me, although I wasn't sure you could call them directions.

"Head back toward Baileyville, and let's see if we can find this place." After we drove for about twenty miles, I thought we ought to be getting close to our next turn. "He said to turn left at Robinson Cut-off. That's about another mile up ahead." I pointed up to the left. "There it is." Tony turned, and we kept going. "Now, we go about three miles. There's a dirt road that veers off where the old Free State Barn used to be."

"How in the world are we supposed to know where a barn once stood that isn't even there any longer?"

"I hope there's something still standing that I will recognize from when I was a kid. My daddy used to bring us up this way to pick blackberries in the spring." I scanned the landscape, looking for any landmarks that I remembered about where the old barn "used" to be. When the mileage showed we'd gone three miles, we saw a dirt road to the right. "There!" I pointed up ahead. "I think that might be it! Turn there and go about another mile. He said all three cabins are around here somewhere. A couple are up here in the woods, but there's one right on the water. I'm betting that's the one Vinnie rented since he was using the boat."

This was the worst road yet, and I was glad Tony had offered his SUV. My Honda was glad, too. About two miles into the woods, we caught sight of the first cabin. It looked empty, but there was a sign nailed to the porch that read: "Jamison #1." We kept slowly making our way, dodging limbs and washed out places in the road till we saw "Jamison #2."

Tony stopped and I got out. I stood next to the car, turning my head this way and that.

He leaned across toward my open door. "What are you doing?"

"There's a fork up ahead, and I was trying to see if I could determine which way leads toward the water."

We stopped talking and listened to the quiet for a minute. I could feel a bit of a breeze, and I felt sure the road to the left led to the water. I wasn't not sure why, but I was gonna go with my gut on this one.

"I say the one to the left. What do you think?"

He shrugged, "Might as well give it a shot."

We got back into the car and began creeping down the fork to the left. After about a half mile, we saw it. There were no cars anywhere around, but I didn't expect to see one. Tony stopped the car.

"Let me do the talking. At least at first, until we see how he's going to react. Family can be unpredictable."

I nodded and let him take the lead as we walked up the steps to the porch. Tony knocked on the door and waited. After a few seconds, he tried again, still with no response.

"Let's walk around back and see if we can see anyone at the dock," I suggested.

We picked our way through the overgrown weeds and bushes to the back of the cabin. From that vantage point, we could see the water and an old boat dock at the bottom of the hill. There was a small fishing boat with a trolling motor tied up at the pier and a small boat shed off to the right, but still no sign of Vinnie.

"If the boat's here, he's got to be around somewhere. How else is he going to get anywhere? Let's go back around to the porch and try again."

Tony knocked one more time with no luck.

"You don't think something's happened to him, do you?" I asked. "Maybe we should just take a peek inside to make sure he's not in there hurt...or worse."

Tony reached for the doorknob, but I grabbed his arm. "Let me do it. If anyone's gonna get in trouble for breaking and entering, I certainly don't want it to be you." He nodded and stepped back.

The knob turned easily in my hand, and I pushed the door open slowly. When I didn't hear any movement inside, I called out, "Hello? Hello? Anybody here?"

When no one answered, we continued into the center of the room. It was a small cabin, really just one large room with a door off the kitchen area which I assumed led to the bath.

"Don't move." A gravelly voice came from behind us. "Who are you and what do you want?" I stood stock still, staring straight ahead until I heard Tony's voice. "Uncle Rocco?"

"Antonio? What are you doing here?" Rocco called Tony by his Christian name. Tony and I slowly turned around, and Rocco lowered the gun to his side.

"What are you doing here, Uncle Rocco? Where is Vinnie?" Tony asked. "Did you kill Gino?"

"You found out he was having an affair with your wife and came down to kill him, didn't you?" I accused.

"Yes. I mean yes... and no," Rocco said, shaking his head.

"I don't understand," Tony stammered. "We were expecting Vinnie to be—"

Just then, the back door flew open and Bianca stood in the doorway, gun drawn. "Put the gun down, Rocco." Her tone was cold and confident.

I swung back around to face her. "Bianca, what are you doing? I thought you were leaving town."

"I would have been long gone, if you hadn't stuck your nose into this. I knew once you said there was someone else from New York in town, I had to follow you and see who it was."

I turned back to Rocco to see his gun pointed at Bianca. Just great. Tony and I were smack dab in the middle of an Italian standoff.

"Uncle Rocco, what's going on?"

"No, Antonio, I didn't kill Gino—she did," Rocco said, still steadily keeping his aim on Bianca. "Yes, I admit I came down here to kill him, but she beat me to it. Angelo sent Vinnie down to protect you."

"Protect me?"

"Yeah, when he found out that Gino was leaning on you and had threatened you about the restaurant, he sent Vinnie down to watch Gino and protect you, should Gino decide to get violent."

"I called Vinnie off and came myself. I had a score to settle with Gino, so I figured I'd come down and protect you and take him out. I realize now, I probably couldn't have gone through with it anyway. He was like a brother to me. No matter what, or who, came between us, we were still family."

I glanced over at Bianca and she still held the gun trained on Rocco, with Tony and me precariously close to the line of fire.

"Once his body showed up at the construction site, Angelo sent word that I was to stay and take out Gino's killer. When I heard she was at the motel, I knew it was her." He gestured toward Bianca with a flip of his head in her direction, the gun never wavered.

"If you are through with your brotherly love sob story, I need to clean up this mess and get on the road out of this deep south sauna. Rocco, if you don't toss the gun, I'm going to shoot your little nephew where he stands."

"Bianca, you don't want to do this. This is between me and you. Let Antonio and this lady go."

"You're crazy if you think I'm going to stand here and go down without a fight. I don't plan on leaving any witnesses."

Rocco suddenly moved to the right to draw her aim away from Tony and me. Bianca fired and Rocco went down, his gun skittering across the floor. Tony dove for Rocco's gun, but Bianca kicked it out of his reach and held her gun to his head.

"Get up and start walking. Both of you. Down to that dock. We're going to take a little boat ride out into the middle of this lake. Unfortunately, I'm the only one who's gonna make it back."

TWENTY

O ne of my greatest fears was suffocation. Nothing struck terror into me more than the thought of drowning. There was no way I was getting into that boat and letting her dump me in the middle of a 260-foot-deep lake. They said there was a forest at the bottom of Smith Lake where the trees were 200 feet tall and the water rose another 60 feet above the treetops. My heart was beating out of my chest as I prayed for a way out of this situation. I prayed for Rocco, hoping that some-how, he would be okay. He lay on the floor of the cabin, not moving. As she forced Tony and me to step over his body to-ward the back door, I tried to see any rise and fall of breathing, but she kept shoving me with the gun in my ribs out into the screened porch. She spotted a roll of duct tape lying on a table with a few other tools.

"You," she said pointing the gun toward me, "tape his wrists together. Do it in the front so he can still tape yours when you're done."

I looked at Tony with my back to Bianca and motioned for him to put his wrists together side by side with palms up, not palms together. I knew that if I taped it loose enough, it would be easier to work our hands free from that position. He took the clue and did what I instructed. I made a huge production of acting like I was taping them tight and tried to keep myself in between Bianca and Tony as much as possible so she couldn't see what a shabby job I was doing.

"Now, you tape hers."

I placed the tape in his hands, and he did the same. She seemed distracted enough to be satisfied with the tape job and shoved us on down the back steps. I still couldn't tell if Rocco was dead or alive.

As we took our sweet time walking down the path to the dock, I deliberately stumbled and fell several times just trying to give me and Tony a few more minutes to live. A few more minutes to come up with a brilliant idea to get us out of this mess.

Then, I made a decision. If she was going to kill me, she would have to work for it. I sat down in the middle of the path. Tony stared at me like I was a loon. Then, he took my cue and sat down beside me. We refused to walk. She could shoot me and drag us both the fifty yards to the boat if she wanted to, but I was *not* going to die in water, never to be found again. So, there we were. Bianca was screaming and we were sitting.

The sun was beginning to set, and it would be dark soon out here in the middle of the forest with no city lights for miles. I wondered if Hunt and Jake would ever find us. I was just so mad at myself for agreeing to let Tony come along. He and Macy would have had a sweet life together. I was heartbroken for her.

"Stop it, Glory. Don't borrow trouble," I could hear my Granny saying.

Just then, I caught a glimpse of Rocco slipping out the back of the cabin, bleeding from his side and barely able to stand. Tony saw him too. Tony and I tried to keep Bianca talking and facing us with her back to the cabin.

"Bianca, Gino didn't really agree to try to work things out with you, did he? That's why you had to kill him."

"Oh, he agreed, alright. Then, when he thought I was asleep, I heard him talking to her, saying, 'Hold off coming down for a few more days, baby, until I can get rid of Bianca. I've talked her into going back to New York and when she leaves to drive home, she's gonna have an unfortunate accident. She'll be out of our way for good and it'll be just the two of us from here on out.'"

She was getting more irate by the second, but hopefully in a few more seconds, Rocco would be close enough to help us. I couldn't see Rocco. I didn't know if he'd made it down the hill or if he'd collapsed from loss of blood. I just figured the longer it took her to get us to the boat, the better chance we'd have. I slowly got up and Tony joined me.

"Stop, Bianca." Rocco stepped out from behind a tree. She spun around and fired the gun wildly. He fired one shot and she was down.

I looked up the hill as an ambulance and several police cars slid to a stop in the dirt outside the cabin. Hunt and Jake jumped out, guns drawn.

"Drop the gun! Get on the ground!" Hunt yelled. "Now!"

As they came barreling down the hill, Rocco dropped his gun and fell to the ground in a heap.

"Hunt, wait!" I screamed.

"It's okay! He's my uncle!" Tony yelled. "He saved us!"

"She's the killer." I lifted both my taped hands toward Bianca, who was lying lifeless on the footpath. One shot. Right between the eyes.

BLUE, RED AND ORANGE lights flashed around us like a night on the midway at the State Fair and the next minutes were a whirlwind of EMTs and a barrage of questions. I leaned against a tree and prayed as we watched the first responders work on Rocco to get him stable enough to transport. I was relieved when I realized that he was responsive.

Jake took Tony's statement while Hunt motioned me over to his department issued truck so I could sit down. He twisted off the top of a cold bottle of water from the cooler in the ambulance and handed it to me. I rubbed at my wrists, where the tape had left raw, red marks, as he started his questions.

He straightened his shoulders and looked down at me while I leaned on the edge of the truck seat. "I'm not even going to try to understand the warped reasoning that allowed you to convince yourself that your little field trip this afternoon was a good idea. I have a feeling that you realize, just a little too late, that it was a foolish thing to do."

I nodded. I would love to have argued with him, but truthfully, I was exhausted, and the worst part was, I knew he was right.

"That being said, start from the beginning and tell me everything."

"First of all, I didn't ask Tony to come along. He insisted. He felt like whoever we found here at the cabin was probably connected to the family, so it would be best if he was here to act as sort of a buffer. It would keep me safer."

"Okay, duly noted. You didn't drag him into your sticky mess. He jumped in of his own accord."

"When we got here and realized it was Rocco that was here and not Vinnie, he was about to explain everything to us when Bianca walked into the cabin. After that, a lot of it is a blur. It was a standoff between the two of them, and she shot him." My voice caught in my throat and I breathed out a long breath. "We didn't know if he was alive or dead." I took a big drink of water and continued.

Hunt rubbed my shoulder, and I shifted to get more comfortable. "Go ahead." He nodded.

"Then, she forced us to tape each other's wrists together and said she was going to take us out into the lake in the boat and dump us in the middle to drown."

I looked down at my hands as they started to shake. The realization began to set in about just how close Tony and I came to dying.

"It's my biggest fear...not being able to breathe. I mean, I'm a good swimmer, but with our hands taped, I don't know how long I could have lasted. My legs aren't as young as they used to be."

Hunt could see I was going into shock and put his arms around me until I could catch my breath and go on. He motioned for one of the officers to bring a blanket from the ambulance.

"I figured, if she was going to kill me, I was going to make her do all the work, so I just sat down and refused to move. I would rather have her shoot me on the path than dump me in the lake. At least y'all would be able to find my body."

Hunt's eyes got big. "That may be one of the smartest plans I've ever heard."

"Well, it wasn't so much a plan as it was just me being obstinate and refusing to cooperate." I smiled.

He chuckled. "I guess that character flaw comes in handy after all."

"Whatever it was, I figured the longer I stalled, the longer we'd be breathing and the better chance we'd have for someone to find us. Which reminds me, how did you know where we were? There's zero service out here. I had promised Macy that I would check in with her when we found the cabin, but I could never get enough service to do it."

"When she didn't hear from you or Tony, she called Jake. I'm just thankful that you had the tracking enabled on your phone, so I could track the signal. We followed it to where you made the last turn into the forest and that's when we lost the signal. From there, we just followed tire tracks."

"I didn't know you could do that." I glanced over and saw that Jake was finished taking Tony's statement and they were walking our way. I watched as the emergency workers were finally able to place Rocco into the back of the ambulance and leave the secluded area on their way to the nearest hospital thirty-five minutes away.

"Are you sure you're okay?" Jake wrapped his arms around my shoulder and hugged me to him.

I nodded and hugged him back. "Tony told me the whole story about the affair between his Aunt Rosie and Gino and how Rocco came down with the intention of killing Gino."

"But Bianca beat him to the punch...or shot, I guess," Hunt added.

"So, does that mean that Uncle Rocco will be free to go back home when he's released from the hospital?" Tony asked.

"I suppose we don't have any reason to hold him. I'm sure there is a crime out there somewhere that he's responsible for, but in this case, ironically, he's the hero."

"After all," I said, "he did save our lives. And he confessed that he probably wouldn't have been able to kill Gino, anyway. They were too close. I could tell that he really didn't want to kill Bianca. I know it sounds crazy, but I think he would've drawn the line at killing a woman if it hadn't been to protect us."

Tony raised his head and looked at all three of us. "If you aren't raised in the 'family', it's hard for people to understand. Honor and family are everything. My dad loves his family, but in his heart, he couldn't justify the lifestyle, so he kept me and my mom as far away from it as he could. Papa Angelo didn't agree, but my dad stood his ground. Over the years, they've only spoken a few times. We keep in touch through my Aunt Celia and she lets us know how they're doing. It's not been an easy life for my parents, but they did it for me."

TWENTY ONE

We walked back up the hill, and Tony and I followed Jake and Hunt back into town. Tony drove, while I took the brunt of Momma's yelling by holding the phone about a mile away from my ear. Tony winced, knowing he was going to get the same or worse from Macy when we got there. The cooking gene wasn't the only thing Macy inherited from Momma.

As expected, Momma, Kelly and Macy were waiting at the bakery. After big hugs all around, they went to fussing, and Tony and I just kept our mouths shut and let them get it out of their systems. Jake and Hunt stood over to the side looking like they were enjoying the sight of me getting my due a little too much. I gave Hunt a pleading look, but he just crossed his arms, smiled and shook his head.

"I just talked to the hospital and Rocco is out of surgery," Tony said, tucking his phone back into his pocket. "Macy and I are headed over there now. I would like to be there when he wakes up."

"Would you mind if I came along? I would really like to thank him." I looked at Macy and Tony.

"I still need to get his statement, so why don't you just ride with me?" Hunt took my hand. "That is, if he's awake and feeling up to it."

Momma looked down at her watch. "It's almost 7:00 now. Why don't Kelly and I head to my house and get some food ready. When y'all finish at the hospital, we'll have some sandwiches and tea for you. I think we all need to 'decompress' as Dr. Phil says on TV."

I laughed at the thought of Momma and her crush on Dr. Phil. "I think that's a great idea, Momma. I don't think it had even registered with me that I hadn't eaten anything solid since breakfast. I'm starved."

Tony and Macy parked in the visitor area at the hospital, and Hunt pulled into the empty space next to them. We walked through the automatic doors and up to the nurse's station.

"Can you tell me where I can find Rocco Castellini? I think he just came out of surgery."

"Are you a family member?" the nurse said, studying her clipboard intently.

"Yes, ma'am. I'm his nephew, Antonio Castellini."

She nodded. "He's just been moved out of recovery and into a room. Room 1422. But you'll need to check with the nurse in charge to see if he's able to have visitors yet. Are all of you together?" She looked me and Hunt up and down with a frown.

"Yes, ma'am. Chief Detective Walker, Sweetwater Police." Hunt flipped open his wallet and showed her his badge.

She took a good look at it and seemed satisfied. "Okay, you can all go through."

Tony slowly pushed open the door to Room 1422. "Uncle Rocco? It's Tony."

I heard the rustling of bedsheets from the other side of the door. "Come in, Antonio." a raspy voice whispered. He looked weak, not the tough guy that had taken charge just a few hours before and taken a bullet for us.

"We know you need to rest, Uncle Rocco, but we just wanted to come and thank you for saving our lives. I know that without your help, Bianca would have gone through with her plan to kill Mrs. Harper and me."

I stepped up to the side of the hospital bed. "I don't think we've officially met, but I'm Glory Harper and this is my daughter, Macy, Tony's girlfriend. Tony is a very special part of our family." I smiled at Tony.

Rocco took my hand in his and patted the top of it with his other hand. "You are a very brave and smart woman, Glory Harper. Not many women I know would have tried what you did today by sitting down on the path to death and refusing to die."

Chills ran down the back of my neck. I hadn't thought about it in those terms. "Rocco, this is Chief Detective Hunt Walker. He was there today, also. He needs to ask you a few questions, if you feel up to it." I took a step away from the bed as Hunt stepped up next to Rocco.

Rocco nodded. "I've answered my share of police questions, I guess a few more won't kill me." He gave a weak grin.

"Glory and Tony have told us what you said in the cabin just before Bianca shot you. Could you clarify for me one more time why you were down here?"

"We've all known about the bad blood between Gino and Tony since Tony left the restaurant business a few years ago." He looked at Tony. "I never got the chance to apologize for getting you into that mess. I should've known Gino couldn't run a legitimate business without dirtying it up with family stuff. It was my fault and you did right pulling out. It took guts and I was proud of you."

He turned back to Hunt. "But I digress. When word got back to Pop that Gino was giving Tony a hard time down here and even threatening him and his business, Pop was blind mad. He was scared that Gino might go too far, so he sent Vinnie down to watch Gino and make sure Tony stayed safe until Gino finished his condo business down here." He scooted himself up in the bed and winced at the pain. "Gino was already on Pop's bad side, since it came out that he was messing around with my wife, Rosie. Pop had disavowed Gino, but Gino thought it would blow over if he just got away for a while and gave it some time."

"So, where did you come into the picture, if he was sending this Vinnie guy?" Hunt asked, steadily taking notes.

"I had a score to settle with Gino, so I called off Vinnie and told him I was coming in his place. I figured I could keep Antonio safe and get rid of Gino at the same time. Everything was going smooth as silk. I rented the boat in Vinnie's name. The guy didn't even check my ID. I just handed him money and he handed me boat keys. Vinnie had already rented the cabin, so he gave me the directions and I was set."

"When did you get here?" Hunt asked.

"I got to the cabin on Sunday night. I was planning on surprising Gino at the motel on Monday night. But, sitting out here in the middle of nowhere, I realized that Gino and I have too much history. He's like a brother, so I decided to just try to talk some sense into him. Get him to go back to Bianca and all would be forgiven."

"When did you find out he was dead?"

"I took the boat back on Monday afternoon to pick up the car and head to the hotel, and I heard the old men at the rental shop talking about a guy found dead at the construction site. I asked if they knew his name and they said all they knew was that he was a "Yankee". I knew immediately it had to be Gino. I called Pop and he didn't say much. I knew he wanted Gino out of the family, but I don't think he wanted him dead. He told me to stay for a few days and see if I could find out who took him out and to take care of them."

Hunt frowned and rubbed his forehead. "Let me get this clear. Your father didn't want Gino dead, but he kicked him out of the family and wanted nothing to do with him. But, when he heard he was dead, he wanted you to take out the person who killed him?"

"I know people who aren't raised in the family don't understand. Honor and family are everything. But family always comes first. Antonio is family and Pop wanted him safe. Gino was like family, so Pop had to avenge his death." Rocco took a slow deep breath and let it out.

"I don't suppose that I can hold you for something that you 'intended to do', so when the doctor releases you to travel, you are free to go. You saved the lives of some people who are very important to me and for that I owe you a debt of gratitude. I can only wish you well and ask that you try to keep 'family' business out of Sweetwater Springs in the future."

"I will do my best. Thank you all for taking care of our Antonio." He looked at Tony and took his hand. "Even though your father and Pop don't speak often, you should know that Pop still loves you all very much and respects your father's decision to keep you away from the 'family'. It's taken him a lot of years to let that go, but he's getting older and he sees what the lifestyle can do to families."

Tony leaned over and hugged his uncle. "Thank you. And please give Papa Angelo my love. I wish you could be here for the grand opening of my new restaurant next week."

"I think it's best if I head back as soon as I am able to drive, but you can be assured that your Papa Angelo will always be watching you. He is so proud of you."

I wondered what he meant by that statement. On second thought, I wasn't not sure I even wanted to know.

We all said our final thank-yous and goodbyes and let him get some much-needed rest.

"I know it's late, but I'm starving. Let's get back to Momma's and dig into those sandwiches."

I suddenly remembered that Macy and Tony had offered to cook supper for us tonight. "Well, Macy, I guess we'll have to take a rain check on that good homecooked meal."

"We'll do it soon. All of seven of us!" she said. "Deal?"

"Deal," Hunt and I said in unison.

Hunt took my hand as we walked back to the parking lot. "Glory, you scared me to death today. I just don't know what I'm gonna do with you."

"I know, I know. I need to think before I go running off to follow a lead. I'll be more careful next time."

"Next time?" his eyes widened. We stopped next to the truck and he opened my door. "You have two part-time jobs. Don't you think that is enough for you to worry about without conducting your investigations behind my back?"

"I'll be glad to conduct them to your face if you'll just share information with me," I quipped.

"How about if we add another job to your resume? Being my full-time girlfriend should fill up any empty slots on your calendar." He smiled, that smile with the dimple.

"Did you ever think that maybe we should go on a real live, full-fledged date before I accept that position? You don't even know me that well. What happens when you realize I'm a crazy, forgetful, impulsive, cooking-challenged..." I paused to take a breath and he jumped in.

"Warm, loving, kind, exciting, ambitious, strong, beautiful woman. I already know all that. Those are the things that drew me to you, and I can't wait to find out more about you. What you love, what you eat, what you listen to, what you read, what you want—"

"Us," I interrupted, reaching over and placing my finger to his lips. "I want us."

He reached over, pulled me to him and kissed me. I breathed in his scent. My heart was pounding out of my chest as I looked into his eyes.

Willing my heart rate to return to normal, I leaned back into the passenger seat and smiled. "I think maybe we need to head on over to Momma's. She's gonna be wondering what happened to us. How about that sandwich?"

"Sure. A sandwich is as good as a steak as long as it's with you, Sherlock."

TWENTY TWO

I was having a major case of déjà vu as we all stood on the Main Street sidewalk, once again smiling for the camera. Our honorable Mayor Jasper Towns snipped the ceremonial ribbon and the doors of Tavolo were officially open to the public.

The night before, Tony had hosted a soft opening by invitation only. The place had been packed with guests including the mayor and city council members, local business owners and friends and family. But as the real guests of honor, Tony had chosen to use this occasion to pay special recognition to our town's first responders. Our police and fire departments, EMTs and those who go to work every day to keep us safe. Jake, Hunt and many others graciously accepted the town's gratitude and praise.

Tony gave a heartfelt welcome and thank you to all who came to help him celebrate his new restaurant.

We enjoyed an authentic Italian meal served "family" style, and by that I don't mean at gunpoint. A crew of servers, wearing white aprons with the restaurant's new logo, brought out bowls and platters piled high with the most delicious pastas, sauces, breads and salads. Tony had done an amazing job. Everything looked so perfect. Music from the Rat Pack era played softly in the background as we passed the dishes around the table. As I looked around our table at Momma, Jake, Kelly,

Macy, and Hunt, Tony walked over and stopped behind Macy, bending down to kiss her on the cheek.

"How is everything? Do you need more bread?"

"Oh, Tony, everything is magnificent. Thank you for giving us the best evening we've enjoyed in a long time," I said. Everyone around the table agreed wholeheartedly.

Tony smiled from ear to ear as he rushed off to check on other guests. I listened to the sounds of clinking glasses, conversations and laughter all over the room as we finished the evening, enjoying every minute of our time together.

I SHOOK MYSELF OUT of the reverie of the night before as Momma, Macy and I headed back into the bakery next door. Several of the onlookers followed us in as the mayor and Tony posed for a few more pictures for the Sweetwater Herald.

I walked over to the display counter as Megan Lester and Cindy Newsome perused the pastries, pointing to each one they were considering and with sounds of "oooh" and "mm-mm."

"Good morning, ladies." I greeted.

"Good morning, Glory," Megan drawled with a warm smile. "I think we'll take two of the apple popovers this morning and a couple of skinny vanilla lattes."

"Y'all have a seat and I'll bring them right over."

"Megan, I heard that there's been some sort of compromise settled on for the condo project. I'm anxious to hear your take on the new plans." I placed their pastries and drinks on the table.

"Yes, Terrance met with the city council along with some of the concerned lake landowners and I do believe, the new proposal is going to benefit everyone."

Cindy nodded. "He's agreed to change his plans for rental condos and turn it into a luxury resort. There will be options to buy properties in the resort, but with the stipulation that they cannot be sublet and no short-term rentals like a timeshare will be allowed."

"According to the ladies down at Bonnie's," I interjected, "it's supposed to include two luxury pools and an upscale restaurant as well as private balconies with beautiful scenic lake views."

"Yes, according to trends in the latest real estate publications, the resort should actually increase the value of our properties," Cindy said, with a smile as she popped the last bite of pastry into her mouth and brushed a stray, flaky crumb from the front of her blouse.

"Well, I hope you ladies have a wonderful day! I'll see you both at the purse auction on Saturday!" Cindy said, scooting her chair away from the table. "We really do appreciate you agreeing to take over the auction after Stephanie had the baby."

"And don't forget our monthly club meeting is next week," Megan added, as she picked up her purse and swung it into the crook of her arm. "Glory, I do hope you'll be ready with your presentation for the Harvest Festival in November. Remember, you volunteered to take the lead on that."

I swallowed hard and forced a smile. "Oh, I have lots of ideas for booths and activities! I can't wait to share them with everyone!" I sure hoped I sounded a lot more confident than I felt.

I waved as they left the bakery and turned to Macy and Momma. "What have I gotten myself into?"

I turned to pick up the plates from the table when I heard the bell over the door.

"Good morning, ladies." Hunt walked over to me, took the dishes from my hands and carried them to the dish bin. "Can we take a walk for a minute?"

"Sure." I cocked one eyebrow and looked at him. "Macy, I'll be back in a few."

"No problem, Mom." She smiled, and I could've sworn I saw her wink at Hunt.

The crowd from just a short time before had finally cleared. I looped my arm through his and snuggled down to keep the wind off as we strolled down the sidewalk.

"I know we need to talk about the whole situation in Texas at some point. I still have a lot of unanswered questions and I know you have some too. Now that I've met you and see first-hand everything you've gone through, I would like to help you get some closure, but only if you think you are up to it. If you want me to drop it, I will. I'll never mention it again. But if you want me to, I still have friends I can trust in the department out there and I could do some digging on the sly."

I could feel the tears welling up in my eyes as I looked up at him. "I know what's done is done. We may never know why things happen like they do. Some things are just not for us to know. But for Macy's sake, it would be nice to have some closure and to know that whoever did this to Dave didn't get away scot free." I stopped walking and turned to face him. "But, listen to me when I say, it is not worth dying for. Do you understand? If this goes as deep as you think it does, promise me you will drop it. I've lost one man. I can't lose another."

He reached over, pulling me to him and kissed me long and hard. It felt like a kiss that meant he was serious about us and had no intention of putting that in jeopardy. "I want to do what it takes to help you get peace about your past, but I refuse to do it at the expense of our future."

Our future. I liked the sound of that.

THE SERIES CONTINUES...

Book 3 in the *Sweetwater Springs Southern Mystery* series is coming soon! Here's a little preview of "*Reunions and Reckonings*".

If you enjoyed reading "*Lakefronts and Larceny*", would you please take a moment to leave a review? It would help me so much! Thank you!

Reunions and Reckonings

Coming May 2020

Francie Baldwin grunted and stretched as she reached to pin the poster to the Community Activities Board on the wall of Macy's on Main. Francie was not a tall woman and she was currently fighting a losing battle with a too-short-for-her-age skirt, yanking it down with one hand and trying to attach the poster with the other. I rushed over to offer my help before she gave Jimmy Don and the table of regulars a coronary.

"Hey, Francie. Can I help?" I offered.

Visibly relaxing down off her tippy-toes, she handed me the poster. "Oh, thank you, Glory. I guess it's a little too high for me to reach." She adjusted her skirt and smiled.

"What's this?" I perused the poster as I secured it to the board. "Class reunion, huh? How exciting!"

"It's gonna be so much fun! I'm on the committee and we're hoping we can have a really good turnout. We're planning it for Homecoming Weekend, so hopefully that will entice everyone to come back."

"That's only a week away, getting kind of a late start, aren't you?"

"This is just a last-minute effort to remind some of the locals. We've already gotten several responses to the invitations we mailed out last month."

"Sweetwater Springs High School Class of '90. Wow, thirty years. Time flies, doesn't it?"

She nodded. "Boy, you can say that again. Seems like yesterday we were living like we didn't have a care in the world. Now look at us. Everybody with kids, families, jobs and mortgages."

"Yes, life sure has a way of moving on, with or without us." I heard a throat clear and saw that the customer smiling from the pastry counter had evidently made her selections and was ready to check out. "Gotta run! Hope y'all have a great time at the reunion!" I waved as she headed out the door, more posters in hand.

"Who was that?" Macy asked, as she breezed through the swinging door from the kitchen.

"Francie Baldwin. Class of '90 is planning a reunion and she was putting up a notice about it." I paused and visibly shivered.

"What's wrong? Do I need to turn up the heat in here?" Macy stood there in short sleeves, sweating from the heat in the kitchen.

"No, I was just thinking about something that happened that year. Class of '90 had a rough go of it their senior year. One of their classmates was killed. It was a terrible tragedy for the whole town."

"Oh, that's so sad. Maybe getting back together to share memories will be good for all of them."

"Maybe. Not everyone's memories are good, though." The bell dinged over the door and I turned my attention to customers.

After crafting a couple of mocha lattes for the two ladies, I grabbed the coffee carafe and headed toward our table of regulars.

"Morning, gentlemen. More coffee?" I circled the table, filling all four mugs being held high in the air. "What's the game today?"

"Scrabble." Otto said. "And I brought my Scrabble Dictionary just to keep this bunch honest. They'd try to cheat their grandmas." He patted the massive volume lying on the table beside him. Otto was a retired attorney and still served on the City Council.

"Hmmph!" Jimmy Don Baker grunted. "I'm the one that has to watch him. He makes up words and then claims they're all legaleeze."

"Well, let's try and keep it civil today!" I laughed.

Billy Franks nudged me as I rounded the table. "Was that Francie Bickerson I saw over there shining all the way to Christmas?"

I snickered under my breath. "Yes, Francie Baldwin, now. She was just putting up a notice about the Class of '90 reunion on Homecoming Weekend. Trying to get the word out, I guess."

"Tsk, tsk, tsk…" Leo Dixon shook his head. "Wasn't that the year the Sanderson girl got killed? Sad, sad, sad." Leo's wife, Bonnie June, was one of Momma's best friends and owner of the gossip mothership we all called Bonnie's Cut and Curl.

"Yes, that's the year. I know because my grandson graduated in that class. Didn't Bradford Jenkins get sent up for that killing?" Jimmy Don asked, more to Otto than the rest of us.

"Yes, Bradford was tried and convicted. Thankfully, I didn't work that case, but I sat in the courtroom and I'm here to tell you, that was one sad day when that sentence was read." Otto said.

"I had just gotten married and moved to Texas when all that happened. I knew it was a bad time for the whole town. But wasn't everybody relieved that her killer was caught?" I asked, pulling up a chair.

"Well, there were more than a few people in town that never believed Bradford killed her. They think he was set up." Billy leaned back on two chair legs.

"Oh, wow. Is he still in prison?" I asked.

"Died last month, I heard. Cancer. I think he was set to be released this year," Otto said.

The door dinged again and in waltzed my two favorite men. My brother, Jake greeted me with a grin and a lift of his chin as he headed straight for the coffee counter and hugged his favorite niece. On the other hand, his boss, Hunt Walker walked straight to me, greeted me with a gaze of his blue-gray eyes and a killer smile with a dimple that made me weak in the knees.

"Good morning, beautiful." He murmured under his breath, so that the customers wouldn't hear.

My face flushed. "Good morning to you," I smiled.

Hunt and I met under unfortunate circumstances when he had to interrogate me about a body that I discovered at a church picnic. That was about six months ago. Thanks to well-meaning family members, we had seen quite a lot of each other at family and community functions over the last few months.

After some very awkward attempts at flirting, we had finally, as of late, become exclusive.

Being a widow who had never dated anyone but my late husband, Dave, this was all new territory to me. Needless to say, my "flirter" was quite rusty. Hunt was a confirmed bachelor, married to the job, as they say, so he was no better at it than me. However awkward it felt, I had fallen hard for him and I hoped that he felt the same. I was finding this extremely private person, a very hard nut to crack. My family and close friends claimed I was an over-sharer. Once I got to know someone, I tended to vomit my entire life story. That's why it had been so hard to keep the one big secret that was lying in my safe deposit box. I'd thought about sharing that with Hunt many times, but it just hadn't felt like the right time yet.

"Do you have plans for the weekend?" He walked beside me back toward the coffee counter.

"I don't know. Do I?" I cocked one eyebrow and smiled.

"I thought we might drive over to Bright City and catch a movie. What do you think?"

"That sounds like fun. I heard about a new Mediterranean restaurant that just opened there. I've been dying to try it!" I said, excitedly.

Hunt wrinkled up his nose. "Mediterranean? Isn't that like a lot of stuff wrapped up in grape leaves?"

I laughed. "Those are called dolmades, and that's only one dish. There are lots of things I bet you would like. My favorite is a traditional gyro. It's a combination of roasted beef and lamb, sliced and wrapped in a soft pita bread. It has lettuce, tomato, onions and a dressing called tzatziki. It's yummy!"

He shrugged one shoulder. "Ummm...that doesn't sound so bad. I guess I can give it a shot. What movie would you like to see?"

"I saw the previews to a new murder mystery that looks exciting."

"Of course, you would choose that." He rolled his eyes. "Do you think that we could see something not quite so closely related to my work and your bad habits?" He was obviously referring to my innate ability to get myself into situations that either put my life in danger or caused him extra stress. On the bright side, I had solved several murders in the last few months. But, as proud as I was of that little accomplishment, he still discouraged my poking around in police business. Go figure.

"Oh, yeah. I didn't think about that." I grabbed my phone from my pocket and pulled up the app for the local movie theatre. "How about comedy or superhero? You choose." I showed him the phone as I scrolled through the app. I figured since he was going to try my suggestion for the restaurant, the least I could do was let him pick the movie.

"We can decide later. Jake and I need to get to the station. We have a conference call from the state office that we can't be late for." He grabbed the cup of dark roast that Macy had poured for him and gave me a wink as they walked out.

RECIPES
Macy's Blueberry Biscuits

S kill Level: Easy Peasy – Makes approx. 12 biscuits

INGREDIENTS:
    2 cups all-purpose flour
    2 tsp. baking powder
    2 tsp. sugar
    ½ stick butter (very cold and cut into pieces)
    ¾ cup buttermilk
    1 egg
    1 cup fresh or frozen blueberries

INSTRUCTIONS:

Mix flour, baking powder and sugar together with a whisk. Cut in butter pieces. Beat egg and milk together in a separate bowl.

Add dry ingredients to egg/milk mixture and mix with a spoon. Carefully fold in blueberries.

Turn out onto floured surface and pat to about ½ inch thick with your hands.

Cut out with biscuit cutter. Place on a sprayed baking sheet with biscuits touching. Bake in preheated 425° oven for 15-20 minutes until biscuits are brown on top.

Glaze Topping: Whisk together 1 cup powdered sugar and 4-5 Tablespoons of milk until you get the consistency you want to drizzle over the biscuits.

Sabrina's Cheddar Garlic Biscuits

S kill Level: Easy Peasy – Makes approx. 12 biscuits

INGREDIENTS:
- 2 cups all-purpose flour
- ½ tsp salt
- 2 tsp baking powder
- ½ tsp baking soda
- 6 T very cold butter
- 1 cup shredded cheddar cheese
- 1 cup (or more) buttermilk
- 1 stick butter (melted)
- 1 tsp garlic powder
- 1 tsp dried parsley

INSTRUCTIONS:

Whisk together flour, salt, baking powder and baking soda in large mixing bowl. Grate cold butter or cut into very small pieces and mix into flour until mixture resembles coarse crumbs.

Stir in cheddar cheese and add buttermilk.

Turn dough onto a floured surface and pat or roll out to about ½ inch thickness. Cut with biscuit cutter of your choice.

Spray a baking sheet with cooking oil and bake in preheated 425° oven for 12-15 minutes.

Mix together melted butter, garlic powder and parsley and brush over hot biscuits as soon as they come out of the oven.

Sabrina's Cheesy Ranch Biscuits

S kill Level: Easy – Makes approx. 12 biscuits

INGREDIENTS:

    2 cups all-purpose flour
    ½ tsp salt
    2 tsp baking powder
    ½ tsp baking soda
    6 T very cold butter
    1 cup shredded cheddar cheese
    1 cup (or more) buttermilk
    1 stick butter (melted)
    ½ package dry ranch seasoning mix

INSTRUCTIONS:

Whisk together flour, salt, baking powder and baking soda in large mixing bowl. Grate cold butter or cut into very small pieces and mix into flour until mixture resembles coarse crumbs.

Stir in cheddar cheese and add buttermilk.

Turn dough onto a floured surface and pat or roll out to about ½ inch thickness. Cut with biscuit cutter of your choice.

Spray a baking sheet with cooking oil and bake in preheated 425° oven for 12-15 minutes.

Mix together melted butter and dry ranch dressing mix and brush over hot biscuits as soon as they come out of the oven.

Glory's Favorite Caprese Quiche

S kill Level: Easy – Serves 8

INGREDIENTS:

    5 large eggs

    5 large egg whites

    1 cup whole milk (2% works too)

    1 cup shredded mozzarella cheese

    2 T fresh basil cut into thin strips

    1 tsp. Garlic salt

    ¼ tsp pepper

    1 or 2 fresh Roma tomatoes thinly sliced.

    1 Deep dish pie crust (frozen or homemade)

INSTRUCTIONS:

Preheat oven to 350°

If using frozen pie crust, place it in the oven for a few minutes until it begins to lightly brown.

Remove and set aside.

Combine all ingredients except tomatoes in a large mixing bowl.

Whisk well and pour into pie crust.

Top with thinly sliced tomatoes and extra basil if desired.

Bake for 45 minutes or until completely set.

About the Author

S.C. Merritt is a Cozy Mystery Author whose stories feature southern female sleuths, plots with a twist and a little sprinkle of romance. The Sweetwater Springs Southern Mys-tery Series is set in a small Alabama town full of quirky charac-ters, delicious restaurants and lots of murder. Yummy recipes are included in each book!

When not writing, she is traveling, watching classic movies and TV shows or collecting flamingos.

She lives in Mississippi with her husband and miniature Schnauzer, Izzy and dreams of living in a tropical locale some-day.

You can find her at: www.scmerritt.com

Amazon: https://www.amazon.com/author/scmerritt

Bookbub:https://www.bookbub.com/authors/s-c-merritt

Facebook: https://www.facebook.com/scmerrittwrites

Follow her on Instagram at: @scmerrittauthor

Follow her on Pinterest at: @scmerrittwrites

Also Available by S.C. Merritt

Sweetwater Springs Southern Mysteries

Potluck and Pandemonium (Book 1)

Lakefronts and Larceny (Book 2)

Reunions and Reckonings (Book 3) May 28, 2020

Moonshine and Murder (Book 4) July 9, 2020